"Wh-what are you doing here?" Kaliah managed, still hoping he wasn't really here at all, and this was all some kind of lurid erotic nightmare.

"Saving you from a sandstorm and ensuring you become my wife—not necessarily in that order," he replied.

Okay, so either she'd lost the plot, or Kamal had.

"You have ten minutes to get dressed and pack what you need while I prepare the horses for our journey," he continued, as if he were the lord of all he surveyed and she his subordinate.

Her rebellious spirit finally kicked in.

"I'm not going anywhere with you," she declared, still shivering, still aching, the dread starting to engulf her.

"This is not a negotiation," he said, his tone tight with strained patience. "If you will not keep yourself and your horse safe, I will do it for you. You now have nine minutes."

Fine, she'd get dressed—because being virtually naked while she confronted him was not a good plan—and then she would tell him where he could stick his rescue and his ludicrous notions of marriage. *Again.*

Meet the Khan family in this series of romances about a ruling desert dynasty, from USA TODAY *bestselling author Heidi Rice.*

Don't miss any of these sexy, contemporary and dramatic romances, set against beautiful, evocative desert settings!

Read Zane and Catherine's story in
Carrying the Sheikh's Baby

Read Raif and Kasia's story in
Claimed for the Desert Prince's Heir

Read Karim and Orla's story in
Innocent's Desert Wedding Contract

Read Dane and Jamilla's story in
Banished Prince to Desert Boss

And meet Kamal and Kaliah in this story
Stolen for His Desert Throne

All available now!

Heidi Rice

STOLEN FOR HIS DESERT THRONE

Recycling programs for this product may not exist in your area.

ISBN-13: 978-1-335-73931-5

Stolen for His Desert Throne

Harlequin Enterprises ULC
22 Adelaide St. West, 41st Floor
Toronto, Ontario M5H 4E3, Canada
www.Harlequin.com

Printed in U.S.A.

USA TODAY bestselling author **Heidi Rice** lives in London, England. She is married with two teenage sons—which gives her rather too much of an insight into the male psyche—and also works as a film journalist. She adores her job, which involves getting swept up in a world of high emotions; sensual excitement; funny, feisty women; sexy, tortured men; and glamorous locations where laundry doesn't exist. Once she turns off her computer, she often does chores—usually involving laundry!

Books by Heidi Rice

Harlequin Presents

Banished Prince to Desert Boss
Revealing Her Best Kept Secret

Billion-Dollar Christmas Confessions

Unwrapping His New York Innocent

Hot Summer Nights with a Billionaire

One Wild Night with Her Enemy

Passionately Ever After...

A Baby to Tame the Wolfe

Secrets of Billionaire Siblings

The Billionaire's Proposition in Paris
The CEO's Impossible Heir

Visit the Author Profile page
at Harlequin.com for more titles.

To all my wonderful readers, with a special shout-out to Carmen, who first put the idea of doing a "second generation" story with Kaliah as the heroine into my head.

CHAPTER ONE

CROWN PRINCE KAMAL ZOKAN, the soon-to-be-crowned King of the Zokari tribal lands, stood in the paddock at Narabia's famed annual horse-racing pageant and scowled as he recalled the meeting the day before with Uttram Aziz, the head of his tribal elders.

The minarets of his neighbour Sheikh Zane Ali Nawari Khan's lavish Golden Palace glittered like jewels in the morning sunshine behind the high stone walls surrounding the stable yards and race arena as flags of every nation fluttered in the breeze and a string of thoroughbred Arabian horses gathered at the starting line. But Kamal could appreciate none of it.

Damn Uttram Aziz. Damn his attempts to defy me at every turn. And, most of all, damn his latest attempt to stop me from claiming my throne.

Adrenaline pumped through Kamal's system as the anger and resentment which had been burning under his breastbone since yesterday's meeting refused to release its stranglehold on his throat.

'It is the law, Kamal. You would know this already if you had a more cultured past. You must be married

before the crowning ceremony next month or you will forfeit the throne.'

Born an outcast boy, he had fought his way from nothing to become Zokar's youngest army colonel, and now—after amassing a fortune by having invested in the country's fledging mineral industry—he was on the verge of becoming its king. The previous Sheikh had died without heirs two months ago and had named Kamal as his successor.

Kamal had no doubt the Sheikh's decision had been based on expediency. Zokar needed inward investment and Kamal was a successful businessman who had also proved himself a leader of men. Kamal had hesitated at first but, once he had decided to take the throne, Aziz and his followers had attempted to thwart him at every turn. And this latest ultimatum had only frustrated him more. How did they come up with this stuff?

Kamal could not have felt more out of place if he had tried, forced to attend Khan's lavish annual event in search of a damned bride. And not just any bride. A royal bride whom, Aziz had stated, would make up for Kamal's lack of breeding and sophistication…

He swallowed, all but choking on his fury. He didn't need breeding, or sophistication, to be a strong ruler and a good king. He was smart, ambitious and determined to obtain the investment Zokar needed to bring its infrastructure into the twenty-first century. He had already invested a small fortune of his own money to that end. But the more conservative elements of the country's ruling elite—represented by Aziz and his acolytes—insisted on putting barriers in his way. Every time Kamal scaled one, there would be another, and he was sick of it.

He glanced up at the royal box where Khan and his brother Prince Raif of the Kholadi people and their families stood with the other local rulers. Kamal shuddered, having escaped from the official greeting ceremony earlier with some excuse about joining his men in the stable yards—where he felt a great deal more comfortable—to watch the main race.

He had respect for Khan. He knew the man had worked hard to develop his kingdom after his father's harsh rule—and Khan had been quick to offer his support when Kamal had been named as successor to the Zokari throne. It was an endorsement Kamal was embarrassed to admit he had needed to smooth his path with the rest of Zokar's tribal elders. Luckily, neither Khan nor his brother Raif had recognised Kamal from their previous meeting fifteen years ago.

But Kamal still remembered the sickening humiliation of that day as if it were yesterday—when he had been a malnourished boy serving the royal party and Khan and his entourage had arrived for a state visit. Kamal had lingered, gathering the dishes as slowly as he could, fascinated by the pride in the powerful sheikh's voice as Khan had introduced his heir—his five-year-old daughter, Crown Princess Kaliah—to the Zokari Elders.

Unfortunately, Kamal had been so intent on eavesdropping on the conversation he hadn't spotted the pillow strewn across his path. He had tripped and dropped the dishes. The crash of breaking porcelain had made every eye turn on him.

Shame washed over him again at the memory of the striking blue of Princess Kaliah Khan's eyes as they had glowed with pity for him. He'd begun gathering the broken pieces, his pride burning, when his employer, Hamid, had appeared, apologising profusely for Kamal's clumsiness, and had proceeded to beat him with his belt.

The vicious swipe had stung like the devil—because the wounds from Kamal's previous beating had yet to fully heal—but not nearly as much as his pride when he'd heard the golden child's impassioned plea to her father. 'Daddy, you must stop that man. He shouldn't hit that poor serving boy, it's not right.'

Poor serving boy?

Khan had intervened, of course, and Hamid had been reprimanded for his behaviour. But the memory of that long-ago encounter still stung. Which was precisely why Kamal had not wanted to come to this event. Being in Khan's debt was bad enough, but the humiliation if he recognised him would be far worse.

At least the Crown Princess was not present in the royal box. The last thing he needed right now was to meet that spoilt, entitled child again—even if she would now be twenty or thereabouts—and risk her recognising him. Although that seemed unlikely. He was six-foot-four now, and twenty-nine years old, even if he felt a great deal older in life experience.

The cool evening air whipped at his skin and the crowd noise increased as the horses took their places behind the starting rope. He swallowed, the fury finally releasing its stranglehold. The rage and pain he had been subjected to as a child had stood him in good stead to ensure he never gave up, and never gave in, before he got what he wanted. Which was why he would scale this latest hurdle and return to Zokar with a willing bride in time to claim the throne once and for all.

His lips twisted in a bitter smile. Hell, he might even consider Kaliah Khan for the position, if she had learned some humility in the intervening years…although he suspected that was doubtful, given her reputation in the region as a wild child.

'Prince Kamal, the Race of Kings is about to start. His Divine Majesty and his wife Queen Catherine would like to welcome you to the royal box with the other heads of state.'

Kamal turned to find one of Khan's many advisers wearing a helpful smile on his weathered face.

'I shall watch the race from here,' he said, knowing he would need more time to prepare for the ordeal of having to socialise at the event scheduled for after the race. Khan and his wife had been welcoming earlier, and surprisingly easy going, but Kamal wasn't a man who knew how to make small talk. Nor did he wish to learn.

The adviser bowed. 'Of course, whatever you wish, Your Highness.'

Kamal turned as the man disappeared back into the crowd, just as a series of shouts came from the paddock. He frowned as a new horse and rider broke into the arena, galloping towards the starting line. The horse was smaller than most of the others, a mare, not a gelding. Kamal couldn't help staring, not just at the horse—whose midnight coat gleamed in the spotlights—but at the rider, who was tall for a jockey but impossibly slender. The way he held himself was spellbinding, so graceful and perfectly attuned with the magnificent horse.

The gun sounded as the new arrival was still racing to join the starting line. The field leapt forward en masse while the trailing horse accelerated as if it had been fired from the gun. The jockey's head was bent low over the powerful beast, his body as one with the animal as its legs ate up the ground.

The crowd went wild, the late horse providing added drama as it flew towards the rest of the field. Kamal's throat clogged as excitement powered through his veins. He had never been much into horse racing—leisure activities were not a part of his life—but even he could admire the poetry of the horse's motion and feel the swell of exhilaration as the horse and rider shot round the first turn without breaking stride, hugging the fence to gain ground on the field.

On the back straight, the horse powered into the lead. But, as the field raced back towards them, the mystery jockey's cap snapped off. Long dark hair fanned out, and Kamal noticed the way the rider's silks flattened in the wind over small, firm breasts.

A woman. What the hell?

As the horse and rider flew past, Kamal got a better look at the jockey's fierce expression—and sensed the effort it was taking for her to stay on the horse.

Fear careered through him.

The horse's speed was completely unchecked. The animal was going too fast, its hooves pounding hard, its flanks sweating with the effort. Was the girl controlling the horse, or was she merely trying to cling onto its back?

That little fool.

Kamal shoved his way through the busy arena stables and leapt onto the nearest saddled horse. Grabbing the reins, he ignored the shouts from the stable hand who had been leading the horse to its stall and charged towards the arena.

The crowds parted to let him through as he galloped towards the track, his mind berating the foolhardy girl even as the fear continued to streak through his body.

The horse was coming down the back straight again as Kamal reached the track. The slender rider was bent so low over the mare now it was clear she had exhausted herself. Adrenaline and something that felt uncomfortably like arousal shot through Kamal as her wild hair flowed around her features, while her slight body clung for dear life to the still accelerating horse.

Kamal spurred his mount onto the track ahead of the runaway mare as it took the turn—determined to rescue the idiot girl before she broke her foolish neck.

'Come on, girl, we've got this.' Excitement barrelled through Kaliah Khan's exhausted body.

We're going to win. And I will finally prove I'm not a total screw-up.

She clung to the reins and kept her body low over

Ashreen's neck, urging her on, aware of all the muscles straining to stay on the horse as they careered around the track. She needed this victory to prove to her family, to prove to Narabia's establishment and to prove to herself she had what it took to win in a man's world.

But most of all to prove to that creep Colin, the guy she'd thought she was falling in love at Cambridge, he'd been wrong to call her a 'frigid bitch'.

Her anger was like an aphrodisiac, turning the fear and danger into exhilaration—and adding much-needed fuel to her flagging stamina. It was as if they were flying. Perhaps if she hadn't been so determined to win she might have controlled the horse more, but it was too late now—Ashreen had scented victory too.

Suddenly an unknown rider on a huge white stallion swerved onto the track ahead of her.

'Who the...?' Liah gasped.

Where had *he* come from? And what was he doing right in front of her?

The horse, much bigger than her mare, picked up speed and moved into her lane, keeping pace with Ashreen's strides. The man was a huge black shadow on the white horse, large and forbidding, powerful and overwhelming.

Liah's shattered mind imagined a Horseman of the Apocalypse come to collect her and take her to hell.

'Get out of the way!' she screamed, but her demand was whipped away on the wind. Her tired arms weighed several tons—all she could do was cling on, her body too weary to manoeuvre Ashreen away from the encroaching rider.

Ashreen lifted her nose, scenting the other animal, and for a split-second Liah was sure the mare would rear, but instead she slowed, almost as if she was intimidated by the huge stallion too.

'No, Ashreen!' Liah shouted. The finish line was just a few hundred metres away. But, before she could get the horse to accelerate again, the rider came alongside her. His hard, angular face was partially covered by a beard, but she could see the fierce concentration in his eyes and the spark of furious temper.

What the heck did he have to be angry about? She was the one getting pushed out of a race she'd been about to win.

'Let go of the reins,' he shouted. 'I'll lift you off her.'

'Are you mad?' she yelled back, but her fingers loosened instinctively.

The air expelled from her lungs in a rush as a hard forearm wrapped around her midriff and she became airborne, plucked from the saddle like a rag doll.

She heard the thunder of Ashreen's hooves as the mare bolted away towards the finish line, leaving her behind. She grunted in shock as she found herself dumped face-down over the rider's saddle. Her stomach slapped down on thighs hard with muscle and she caught a lungful of his scent—spice, musk and clean soap. His robe wrapped around them both as the mighty horse reared. But Liah didn't even have a chance to scream before the horse bowed to its rider's commands and its hooves crashed back to earth, giving her stomach another painful jolt against those rock-solid thighs.

His hand remained firm on her back, keeping her in

place as he steered the horse across the track, bringing them to a stop inches from the fence.

The crowd erupted, waving and cheering, as if the whole thing had been planned for their entertainment. Nausea boiled in Liah's stomach, her mind reeling as the giddy adrenaline rush slammed into a wave of shock and fury.

What had just happened? And who was this mad man? Because he'd nearly killed them both…and, more importantly—he'd just lost her the race. Every part of her body throbbed with pain. But what hurt most of all was her pride.

The rest of the field raced past them as the man dragged her up to seat her across his lap so she could see his face. Dark brows flattened over piercing golden eyes which looked weirdly familiar. Had she seen this man before? Because those amber eyes struck something in her memory from long ago.

But nothing else about him seemed familiar. And she was immediately struck by the thought that, if she had met him before, she would not have forgotten him.

He was huge, all hard, lean muscle, a brutal scar slashed down his left cheek creating a raised line through the stubble on his jaw. The fierce intensity as his gaze raked over her made the harsh planes and angles of his sun-weathered features look even more dramatic.

He wasn't what she would call handsome, his dark, raw-boned face far too intimidating and defiantly masculine for that, but he was breath-taking.

And hot.

Liah stifled the idiotic thought as unhelpful heat joined the bubble of nausea in her belly.

'You are not hurt?' he asked, his rough, heavily accented voice echoing in her chest—and triggering the pulse of something rich and fluid in her sore abdomen.

The question jolted her out of her trance—and drop-kicked her back into reality.

She pushed against his controlling arm. 'Of course I'm not hurt,' she said, her voice coming out on an annoying squeak. She gathered another breath. 'No thanks to you, you idiot. What on earth were you thinking, grabbing me like that? You could have broken both our necks.'

His dark brows lowered and anger sparked, turning the rich amber in his gaze to a flaming gold. 'I saved your life, you ungrateful little fool,' he snapped, his voice rigid with condescension.

Liah's temper burned through the last of her shock and misplaced awe.

'Are—are you deranged?' she spluttered, barely able to contain her incredulity at the arrogant statement. 'I was about to win.'

'The horse was out of control,' he said. 'And you were too weak to manage it.'

Weak? Weak!

She heard it then, the note of masculine disdain she had been battling from some quarters all her life, despite the unstinting support of her parents and Narabia's ruling council.

She swept the mane of unruly hair out of her eyes. 'I get it, you decided to rescue me when I didn't need rescuing because I'm a weak and feeble woman, right?' She glared at him with enough force to immolate lead.

Unfortunately, it had no appreciable effect. He didn't even have the decency to flinch before giving her an insulting once-over—which, infuriatingly, had that inappropriate shaft of heat returning.

'You are a woman?' He sneered, the rhetorical question dripping with sarcasm. 'This is hard to tell when you are dressed like a boy. And behave like a spoilt brat.'

Her temper shot straight to boiling point without passing go. She sucked in an agonising breath of outrage, the urge to punch the contemptuous look off his face so strong she had to force herself to breathe through the fury.

She had never struck another human being in her entire life and she did not plan to start now. Especially as his rough-hewn jaw looked so solid, it would probably break all her fingers if she tried. But it was a major battle to keep her tightly balled fists by her sides.

She broke eye contact first, but then the brutal humiliation returned full force as she spotted her father striding towards them through the crowd. Her mother followed, looking concerned. As the crowd parted for their sheikh, it occurred to Liah the spectators—the people she was one day supposed to govern—had been listening to every word of her exchange with the man holding her on his lap.

Terrific. How on earth am I going to regain any semblance of respect after this?

'Let me down,' she insisted, pushing at his controlling arm. She did not want to face her father's wrath while sitting on this man's lap. Her pride had already taken a direct hit, thanks to him. But, instead of releasing her, the jerk's muscular forearm tightened, keeping her in place with embarrassing ease.

Wrestling with him would only make it worse, so she was still stuck on his horse when her father reached them. She spotted the tight muscle in her father's jaw ticking like a demented metronome—a sure sign she had gone too far and was in serious trouble. She only prayed he would not break his golden rule and chastise her in public.

Her mother touched her father's arm and murmured something to him.

Liah felt the air in her lungs release as her father drew himself back from the edge—her mother had always been able to work miracles on her father's temper. But his gaze flicked over her with enough derision to make her shudder before he addressed the man behind her.

'Prince Kamal, my wife and I can only thank you for rescuing my daughter,' he said, his voice clipped and curt.

Prince? This guy was a prince? *Seriously?* A prince of where? He looked—and had behaved—more like a bandit.

'He didn't rescue…' she began, but her father simply lifted his hand.

'Don't,' he said, the single word loaded with enough barely leashed fury to silence her instantly. 'Go and change into your outfit for tonight's reception, Kaliah,' he said, his tone going from chilled to freezing.

'And we can discuss this…' he paused, the muscle ticking over time '…this *situation* later, once I have had a chance to thank the prince properly.'

Which was clearly code for, *Get to the palace before I lose my cool once and for all.*

She bit her lip to stop the passionate defence of her actions spewing out of her mouth as impotent fury boiled in her sore stomach. If this jerk hadn't 'rescued' her, she would have won the race and her father would have understood why she had risked her personal safety. Instead of which, she just looked like even more of a monumental screw-up.

'I would,' she managed at last. 'Except he won't let me off his horse.'

'Perhaps if you had asked me politely,' the bandit prince interjected, 'I would have considered it, Your Highness.'

She spotted the mocking twinkle in his golden eyes and the twitch of his hard lips.

Indignation blind-sided her. *The rat.* He was actually enjoying this, getting off on making a fool of her in front of her father, her mother and all their subjects.

She forced herself not to rise to the bait. Everyone was still watching, and she would be the bigger person now if it killed her…which, judging from the pain in her chest as she struggled to breathe past her fury, might actually happen.

'Please, Mighty Prince Kamal,' she said, fluttering her eyelashes as if she were the simpering idiot he obviously took her for. 'Could you let me off your horse?'

Before I punch you.

The amusement in his eyes flared. A strange tingling sensation ran riot over her tired, sore body, waking up parts of her anatomy she did not want awakened and making her far too aware of the rock-hewn thighs beneath her bottom.

What on earth was that even about? Because she already couldn't stand this man and she'd only just met him.

Without another word, his muscular forearm released its hold on her stomach. She jumped down from the horse with as much dignity as she could possibly muster while her temper was still boiling and her legs had turned to mush. Everyone—her father included—was watching her as if she were a naughty child now instead of a princess.

Locking her knees, she forced her chin up and began her walk of shame. But, as she made her way through the parted crowd towards the palace, she could feel the Jerk Prince's mocking grin following her. Awareness rioted over her skin at the sudden thought of his fierce amber gaze sinking to her backside.

What the heck?

Her walk of shame turned into the seventh circle of hell as she bit into her lip hard enough to taste blood.

CHAPTER TWO

'DAD, YOU CANNOT be serious? The man is an arrogant, sexist jerk—who basically robbed me and Ashreen of the victory we've been training for for months. I don't want to spend ten seconds in his company let alone the whole evening as his personal tour guide.' Liah stared at her father, trying to keep the pleading note out of her voice.

But the punishment he had devised was too much. Even for him. She'd actually rather die than shepherd Prince Kamal around tonight's reception. Especially as he'd probably use the opportunity to be even more of an overbearing ass.

Her father's eyes narrowed as he looked up from his desk. 'Which is precisely why I want you to do it,' he said, being about as flexible as a lump of rock.

'But I—'

'Enough of the *I*!' He cut her off. 'Not everything is about you, Liah. This is the first time Prince Kamal has ventured out of Zokar after being named as the heir to the throne. He seemed ill at ease in the royal box earlier. He's ruling a country that is one of our nearest neighbours—and he has a background which hasn't prepared him for events like tonight's.'

What background? The question popped into Liah's head. She shoved it right back out again. She wasn't interested in the man or his background.

'As the Crown Princess, it is your job to make him feel welcome,' her father added.

Liah's belly tightened into a knot at the disappointment in her father's tone, which struck at all her insecurities.

Her father was a brilliant ruler who had dedicated his life to Narabia. He and her mother had been instrumental in helping to evolve the country's culture and traditions in the last twenty years so everyone had access to education and health care. Declaring their daughter as heir to the throne, when Liah had been their first born, instead of waiting for a son, had been an important part of that. But how did she tell them both, when they had always had such faith in her, that she had no faith in herself?

She didn't want to let Narabia or them down but, while she agreed with her father one hundred percent that a woman could rule the country just as well as a man, deep down she wasn't convinced she was that woman.

Her parents had always ruled her brothers and her as they ruled the kingdom—by consent. They'd allowed Liah to spend her childhood summers in Kildare, at her cousins' stud farm, because of her love of horses. And had allowed her to study in the US and the UK when she'd asked.

The problem was, she had always been impulsive and headstrong…and she couldn't seem to change that part of her nature, not even for them, no matter how hard she tried.

She sighed, trying not to let the creeping feeling of inadequacy show. If there was one thing she'd rather die than lose, it was her father's respect.

'Fine, I'll do it,' she conceded. 'But I'm only doing it because you've asked me to. I still think Prince Kamal is a jerk and that I did not need rescuing.'

'I know.' Her father's lips quirked, creating a crack in his stern expression. He masked it instantly, but the knot in her belly loosened. She knew she exasperated him a lot of the time. They exasperated each other, probably because they were so alike. But she also knew he loved her, fiercely and without compromise. And that would never change, no matter how many times she screwed up.

Thank goodness.

'You're an exceptional horsewoman, Liah,' her father added. 'And, maybe if your mother and I had known you'd been working with Ashreen ever since you returned from college, we wouldn't have both shaved several years off our lives watching you shoot round that track as if you had wings…'

She heard the pride in his voice, which had always been there, ever since she'd been a little girl and he'd believed she could do anything if she put her mind to it. 'But if you ever do anything like that again,' he continued, thrusting his fingers through his thick dark hair, the strands of grey at the temples making him look even more distinguished than he had when she'd been a child, 'I may have to ground you for the rest of your life.'

'Point taken.' She huffed out a laugh. It was an empty threat. They both knew it. But she could hear his anxiety.

Okay, she owed him one.

'I promise I'll be the perfect hostess with Prince Kamal this evening.' *Aka Prince Rat.* 'And I'll do my absolute best not to tell him what an ass he is,' she added, which, in all honesty, would require every molecule of self-restraint she possessed.

Kamal heard the knock on the door and swore under his breath as he stared at the scrap of black cloth hanging limply around his neck. It would probably be one of Khan's staff waiting to escort him to the event downstairs.

The event he did not wish to attend—at all.

The black tuxedo trousers and fitted white shirt had been expertly tailored to fit his muscular frame, but still he felt like a fraud. He was not used to formal western evening wear, much preferring the loose robes of the desert. But he knew he needed to become accustomed to such things for the European trade tour he had planned as a precursor to his coronation. Assuming, of course, he could find himself a convenient bride.

He scowled at his reflection in the floor-length mirror. At least the trousers and shirt had been straightforward. The tie, though, had completely confounded him. Khan's wife had offered to supply him with some-

one to help him dress, but he had declined, thinking
the concept absurd—he had been dressing himself for
as long as he could remember. Now he wished he had
not been so hasty.

The knock sounded again.

He marched through the suite of rooms to the door,
the last of his patience evaporating.

He swung open the heavy oak door. 'Yes?'

The vicious spear of lust he had been suppressing all
evening—ever since Princess Kaliah had been wrig-
gling on his lap—shot back into his groin.

Her. Again. This time not dressed as a jockey but as
a princess. A nearly naked princess.

A stunning red satin creation draped down to her
ankles, but had a plunging neckline and a slit up one
side which highlighted her modest cleavage and mile-
long legs, while the jewelled shoulder-straps appeared
flimsy enough to snap at any minute. His gaze swept
over her, from the artfully arranged curls piled on top
of her head to the peak of painted toes in heeled san-
dals.

She cleared her throat and his gaze jerked to her
face. Her sapphire eyes had been enhanced by some
kind of glittery, smoky stuff, while her full lips glis-
tened in the dim lighting of the palace's courtyard,
making them look even more kissable.

'Prince Kamal, I presume?' she began, her voice a
little breathless.

He knew how she felt. He had not been expecting
her—and especially not dressed like *this*. She certainly

did not look like a boy any more. Not that she ever really had.

'What do you want?' he asked more rudely than he had intended. But she had him at a disadvantage, the uncomfortable awareness from earlier now turbocharged, and he did not like it.

If he had briefly entertained the idea Princess Kaliah might be a possible candidate to become his queen, he had dismissed the thought as soon as he had realised who was the rider he had rescued.

As much as he had enjoyed getting some payback for the long-ago humiliation he had suffered at her hands—and watching her ice blue irises turn to hot steel while she'd attempted to struggle out of his lap—he had also realised the princess's reputation as a wild child had been well-earned. Kaliah Khan was clearly completely undisciplined, headstrong and spoilt. He needed a queen who would do as he told her, who would respect his authority and be a good role model, not an unruly girl who seemed to have no control over her behaviour whatsoever.

So proposing to her was out.

His gaze raked over the revealing dress again. Not only was her reckless behaviour a problem but he also doubted she was a virgin. She was far too confident and aware of her sexual allure. And, while he didn't much care for the double standard required of him in his position, he had no intention of offering for a woman who was not untouched. He was not about to give Uttram Aziz and the other more conservative elders a chance to reject his bride on a technicality.

He could see the spark of temper in her eyes now, but she masked it—mostly—before she replied, her voice an annoyingly husky purr. 'My father requested that I escort you to the reception and introduce you to the other guests.'

So she was here under duress. It figured.

'Requested or demanded?' he asked.

Surely she had no wish to accompany him any more than he wished to have her as his guide? He had enjoyed baiting her earlier. But the payback he had wanted had now been fulfilled.

As she had left the arena, haughty fury emanating from each regal stride, he had been unable to unglue his gaze from her pert backside. Which was problematic, because he had already dismissed her as a prospect for marriage.

He also recalled now how she had felt on his lap, her back rigid, her breasts rising and falling in an erratic rhythm beneath the jockey silks, her wild hair clinging to the graceful line of her neck, and also recalled the scent of her—the musty spice of subtle perfume and female sweat, all but addictive.

And now here she was again, looking stunning. The unwanted heat settled back in his groin on cue.

Kaliah Khan—and her strident beauty—was a distraction he did not need while he looked for a biddable woman to propose to this weekend.

She sent him a flat look and placed a clenched fist on her hip, making the gown's fabric skim her cleavage in a way that had his mouth watering involuntarily.

'Demanded, actually,' she replied, her brutal honesty gaining his grudging respect. 'But I'm willing to overlook your ruining my chances of winning the race.' She bit the words off, her temper making those pure blue eyes sparkle like the jewels in her intricately beaded hair. 'So I can help you out tonight. My father says you don't know anyone, that you're not used to this kind of event, and he wants you to feel welcomed and at ease.'

His back stiffened. He could hear only irritation in her tone at her father's demand, rather than condescension, but he had spent enough of his life being looked down on to detect it nonetheless.

Having spent twenty minutes wrestling with the idiotic piece of fabric around his neck, he was not about to be bested by this spoilt young woman.

'Tell His Divine Majesty that I appreciate it,' he said, making it very clear he did not appreciate it. 'But I do not require the help of someone who believes herself above me.'

He stepped back, intending to shut the door, glad to have the last word and expecting her to be glad she would not have to spend the night in his company. But, to his surprise, she slapped her hand against the heavy oak. The irritation had left her eyes to be replaced by what could only be described as curiosity.

'Wait—what gave you the impression I think I'm above you?' she asked, the question apparently a genuine one.

Because you were born royal. And I was born a nobody.

He cut off the errant thought ruthlessly. The acci-

dent of his birth did not make him beneath any man...
or any woman.

Feeling annoyed and exposed, he propped his shoulder against the door frame, crossed his arms over his
chest and glared at her.

'Is this not the case?' he asked, determined to regain the high ground. 'When we met earlier, you did
not speak to me with respect.'

To his surprise, instead of saying what he had expected—that of course she was better than him—a
line appeared between her brows and her gaze soft-
ened, making the deep blue glow with something that
looked oddly like embarrassment.

'Well, to be fair, you didn't exactly talk to me with
much respect either,' she said. Before he could counter her observation, she added, 'That said, I was angry
with you earlier for rescuing me when I didn't need rescuing. But, if I gave you the impression I was angry at
you for some other reason, I apologise. Believe me, I
don't think I'm above anyone. And, at the moment, my
father would certainly agree with me on that score.'

He straightened from the door frame, so surprised
by the candid comment and what sounded like genuine
regret that he was momentarily disconcerted.

Surely it had to be a trick?

But somehow, he couldn't seem to throw her art-
less apology back in her face. Because it was the first
he had ever received from someone of her status. The
pulse of emotion in his chest was ruthlessly quashed,
though. Sentimentality had no place in his life. And he
certainly did not *require* an apology from her or any-

one else. He had stopped caring what people thought of him a long time ago.

'If you are genuinely sorry, perhaps you could show me how to deal with this.' He flicked the offending tie. Maybe she could be useful after all. 'Do you know what is supposed to be done with such a pointless thing?'

She nodded, clearly willing to accept the uncomfortable truce. Then, to his surprise, she sashayed past him into the suite of rooms. The swish of her skirt sent a waft of the subtle, refreshing perfume through his system again…and gave him a disturbing view of her naked back. The damned gown plunged down to the curve of her backside, and his gaze snagged on the round orbs again, which looked like two ripe plums ready to be plucked.

He forced his gaze to her flushed face as she swung round to face him.

'Okay, you'd better close the door,' she said, the guileless look in her eyes suggesting she had no idea how that request would make the heat pulse in his groin. 'I'm not exactly an expert myself on bow-ties, but I've helped out my younger brothers a few times, so I'll give it my best shot.'

He found himself closing the door against all his better instincts. But, as she reached up on tiptoe to grasp the two ends of fabric, he tensed. 'What are you doing?' he growled, his voice a rusty purr.

Good God, was she trying to unman him?

She stood so close, the gown brushed his legs and he could see the outer edges of her breasts. Was she even wearing a bra? How did her breasts remain inside the gown—surely they could fall out at any moment?

Her gaze rose to his, her golden skin darkening as she blushed. Her blue eyes were guileless—but also round with curiosity. 'Tying your bow-tie,' she said. 'What did you think I was going to do—ravage you?'

Liah cursed the loaded question as soon as it left her lips.

Why did she always have to say exactly what she thought? And what on earth had she been thinking, strolling so casually into this man's suite? Because, now she was standing in the large lavishly furnished living area, alone with him, it felt far too…dangerous.

She stepped back, aware of the dark intensity in his gaze and the heat emanating off his muscular frame.

She'd been instantly overwhelmed as soon as he'd flung open his door with that harsh look on his hard, angular features. Which was of course why she'd begun babbling inanely—and trying to assert herself.

She hadn't expected him to open his own door. And certainly had not been prepared for the sight of him in dress trousers and a fitted white shirt, the dark hair on his chest visible through the expensive linen. The untied bow-tie draped casually around his neck, the small nick on his chin where he must have cut himself shaving and the delicious aroma of sandalwood soap and clean male had only added to the strange sense of intimacy and sensory overload.

As his gaze had raked over her—with ruthless entitlement—she'd suddenly felt naked, her dress choice ill-advised, to say the least.

She loved the designer gown, adoring the way it draped over her slender curves and made her look less boyish—but she felt a bit too much of a woman right now.

A woman this man could probably devour in a heartbeat if he chose…

Not that she wanted him to. Not at all, she told herself staunchly, even if her knees felt a lot less solid than usual and as though a hot, heavy rock had dropped into her abdomen and started to glow.

He was still staring at her. But, instead of answering her beyond stupid question, he simply inclined his head slightly.

'No,' he said. 'Proceed,' he added, like a man who was used to giving orders and having them obeyed.

So much for her father's assertion that Prince Kamal was uncomfortable about his role, because to her he seemed to be a natural born ruler.

She was forced to step closer to him again.

The strong brown column of his throat flexed as he swallowed. Inappropriate moisture flooded her panties as she slipped her fingers under his collar to hook the top button on his dress shirt.

He huffed.

'Is everything okay?' she asked, feeling oddly as if she were trying to calm a highly strung stallion, a wild one that could stamp her to dust at any moment.

His golden gaze met hers. 'It feels as if I am being strangled.'

'Sorry,' she murmured. 'It's necessary to have the collar buttoned to tie the bow-tie.'

He nodded, but she could see in his eyes he was unimpressed.

Lifting on tiptoes, she grasped the ends of the tie, cursing her trembling fingers, her curiosity piqued again. The way it had been moments before when he had accused her of disrespecting him with that jaded, deliberately unconcerned look on his face, as if he was used to such treatment. A million questions rose to the surface of her brain, questions she knew she shouldn't indulge, but even so…

Why had he never worn a tuxedo and bow-tie before? How had he gained the throne of Zokar? What *was* his background—the background her father had referred to as not having prepared him for events like the one which had already started downstairs? Where had he got that scar? And why did his golden gaze seem somehow familiar?

She chewed her lip to stop the intrusive questions coming out of her mouth and concentrated on tying his bow-tie while preventing her knuckles from brushing against the warm skin of his throat.

One thing was for sure—doing this service for her two youngest brothers, Kasim and Rohaan, was nowhere near as nerve-racking, even though neither one of them could stand still for more than a nanosecond.

After several endless minutes of torture, she managed to arrange the bow-tie into some semblance of order.

'There, that's it, I think,' she said, dropping her hands and scooting back.

She glanced up to find him watching her. His golden

gaze was assessing, focussed and full of something hot and intense—which for once did not look like animosity.

A wave of warmth spread up her neck, making her far too aware she had only the stick-on bra cups under her dress to stop her puppies falling out of the daring gown.

'How does it feel?' she asked, determined to break the strange spell.

He touched the tie, shifted it slightly then stretched his neck. 'Uncomfortable.'

'You've never worn one before?' The question popped out.

His jaw tightened. Had she offended him again?

But his gaze remained direct as he gave a curt shake of his head.

'There was no need for such nonsense in the Zokari army,' he explained.

There was distain in his tone, but she found his reply refreshingly blunt. An appreciative laugh burst out of her mouth.

'Just be glad you don't have to do this in ridiculous footwear too,' she said, extending her leg to show him her four-inch heels.

His gaze roamed over her thigh and down to her ankle, blazing a trail along her flesh.

'Elegant,' he murmured.

The gruff compliment reverberated through her torso as his gaze finally arrived back at her face.

She hastily draped the satin back over her leg.

Good grief, Liah, why not give him an eyeful of all your charms?

She couldn't prevent the shudder as the heat centred in her core.

He lifted a black tailored jacket off the back of a chair, slipped it on then did up one of the buttons, completing the devastating effect.

He really did look spectacular, his dark skin and rugged features as striking as they were intimidating. The formal wear only seemed to enhance his raw masculinity, the aura of command which clung to him. Whatever his background, it was clear he was a man used to commanding men…and no doubt women too.

But not this woman. You're your own woman, Liah. Remember that.

She squeezed her thighs together, determined to ignore the insistent pulse that had centred between them.

Then, to her surprise, he offered her his elbow. 'Let's get this over with before the foolish thing strangles me.'

Another chuckle escaped her lips. But the hot blast of appreciation in his gaze as she touched his muscular forearm and felt it tense beneath the expensive fabric choked the laugh off in her throat.

CHAPTER THREE

SHE IS FASCINATING. And I want her.

Kamal found himself staring again at the young woman beside him, who was chatting with considerable authority about her horse Ashreen to the Queen of Zafar, an Irish woman who he understood was a cousin of the royal family by marriage and owned a world-renowned racing stud in Kildare.

Princess Kaliah's passion for the subject of horses and racing was evident in the way her eyes gleamed, and her tawny skin literally glowed with enthusiasm.

She had remained by his side throughout the evening, introducing him to everyone and talking with depth and knowledge on a variety of topics, both trivial and complex. She had made an effort to involve him in these conversations—and for once he had not found her interventions condescending or annoying. In truth, she had beguiled him.

He knew she was being so attentive to please her father, but to his surprise she had not shirked the responsibility as soon as she could. Instead, she appeared to be working overtime to put him at his ease.

Good luck with that.

How could he be at ease when he kept catching her intoxicating scent, and while tantalising glimpses of her unfettered breasts, moving against the line of her gown, and her toned thigh every time she walked, was driving him insane.

Would it really be so wrong to seduce her before I start searching for a suitable wife?

The errant thought made the slow burn in his gut flare.

Probably not a good idea. For all her wild-child ways, Kaliah Khan was a future queen. The sort of woman who would have expectations he could not fulfil.

Although, to his surprise this evening, she had been forthright—including him in the joke, rather than attempting to make him the butt of it.

As much as he still wanted to resent the reckless young woman who had railed at him at the race track, he was finding it harder and harder not to notice her passionate response to him.

Women had always been straightforward to him—a means of slaking his physical needs, but little else. He had never conducted an in-depth conversation with any of the women he had slept with, because all he had ever needed was confirmation that they were happy to tumble into his bed for the night.

Kaliah Khan, though, was an enigma. Her obvious interest in him was both captivating but also somehow unclear—the woman had been reckless enough to ride a virtually wild horse at breakneck speed, so her reticence now made no sense to him.

Hence the intriguing mystery she represented.

He had seen the flush of awareness back in his suite, and had suspected the decision to help him with the bow-tie had been a means of flirting with him. Perhaps even to tease him, the casual brush of her fingers on his throat enough to tie his guts in knots for the rest of the evening. But he sensed innocence, rather than calculation, every time he caught her watching him.

She liked what she saw too, but had remained business-like since leaving his suite.

But, the more she attempted to hide her attraction, the more he found himself wanting to force her to acknowledge it.

Again, not wise. As she was the wrong woman, at the wrong time, in the wrong place.

Perhaps there remained some of that invisible serving boy still inside him who would never have been good enough for a woman like her—making the desire to bed her all the more fierce.

He could have any woman he wanted now. But tonight there was only one woman he wished to have. He'd enjoyed watching her interact with the many pointless people at this reception, but it was past time to show her he could see her interest in him and that he returned it.

They only had tonight to see where this chemistry might take them, before he would have to spend the rest of the weekend looking for a wife.

'It was lovely to meet you, Prince Kamal.' The Queen

of Zafar broke off her discussion with Kaliah to address him directly. 'I do hope you will consider visiting us in Kildare when you are in Ireland on the trade tour,' she added.

He nodded, surprised she knew about the tour, which he had only finalised a week ago.

'Thank you for the invitation,' he said, making no commitments. The need to find himself a wife had to be his first priority or there would be no tour.

Resentment at the thought of his predicament tightened his throat, as Queen Orla left them.

Princess Kaliah turned to him, her gaze probing. 'Why didn't you accept her invitation?' she asked, the question abrupt and intrusive. 'Orla and Karim are an important power couple in the region, and they also have a high profile in Europe.'

He bristled at the suggestion he could not navigate the social commitments of a king. The surge of heat, which had been tormenting him every time he looked at her, only intensified his resentment. He should not have stayed by her side all evening but should have been acquainting himself with the more suitable women here he was required to seduce.

'And this is your business how, exactly?' he snapped, his frustration building as her breasts pressed against the edge of her gown, and he imagined drawing the fabric aside so he could finally look his fill.

She blinked, her skin flushing. 'Are you naturally surly, or is it just me?' she asked, the bold question tempered by the vulnerability in her eyes.

She masked it quickly, but even so it made the heat

ignite. He wanted her, and she wanted him. Why deny this attraction, when it would be simple enough to feed?

He stepped closer, touched a knuckle under her chin and felt her gratifying shudder of response. 'It is most definitely just you, Kaliah.'

Her eyes widened, then darkened with awareness. The heat in his groin throbbed.

She didn't say anything. He let out a rough chuckle. Was she trying to be demure?

He swept his thumb across her bottom lip, then let his hand drop. He would never pressure her physically. But he went after what he wanted. And tonight he wanted her.

'Perhaps we could go somewhere less public to discuss it?' he suggested.

The vivid blush on her cheeks heightened. He had been too blunt. But he was damned if he would pretend to be someone he was not—a man with finesse and fancy manners.

As he waited for her response, transparent emotions skittered across her expressive features—shock, indignation and then a vivid, vibrant curiosity. The heat in his groin swelled against the confines of his suit trousers. Why did the fact she was so transparent only make her more alluring to him?

But, just when he was convinced she would tell him to get lost, her answer came out on a throaty purr. 'Okay.'

He threaded his fingers through hers and led her through the throng of people. As his grip tightened, he forced himself not to walk too quickly. But as they made their way through the large palace atrium and into a quieter courtyard, where a fountain surrounded by tropical blooms gave the dry desert night the sultry scent of flowers, his heartbeat accelerated.

The crowds of guests melted away as they reached the staircase to the private terrace where his suite of rooms was situated. He made himself take the steps one at a time, although the desire to lift her into his arms was all but overwhelming. Especially as the sound of her harsh breathing matched the vicious pump of his pulse.

Perhaps he should say something to put her at her ease. But he had never been a man for pointless conversation, especially now, when the desire that had been kept at bay so ruthlessly all evening was ready to burst its bounds.

He wished to make this good for both of them. And for that to happen he needed to concentrate on keeping his hunger in check before he got her naked.

So he remained silent and led her into the night.

You need to stop this madness, Liah, before it's too late. You don't even know this man. You're not even sure you like him.

Even as she struggled to keep up with Kamal's forceful strides, the hum of conversation and music fading as he led her through the dark corridors towards his suite, Liah couldn't seem to stop the buzz of attraction sinking deep into her sex.

Where had that insistent throb come from that had

made her so brutally aware of this man? Even though he had been silent, bordering on rude, all evening. He'd barely spoken to any of the people she had introduced him to. He'd made no real effort to enter into the sort of polite conversations that were a requisite of these events.

She had wondered more than once what he was thinking behind those fathomless eyes. Was he judging her—judging all of them? It was clear he thought the whole event frivolous and—even though she would normally have agreed with him—she had found herself wanting to defend her way of life.

She should have left him to his own devices hours ago because almost as soon as they had arrived at the reception it had been clear that, although Prince Kamal knew virtually no one here, he didn't need her help to smooth his path because he had no desire to fit in.

But his apparent disdain had done nothing to dispel the deep pulsing need that she now realised had been tormenting her ever since he had plucked her off Ashreen and draped her over his lap without even breaking a sweat.

Since when had she been attracted to overbearing, arrogant men? All her previous boyfriends had been intellectual, bordering on nerdy. Was that why they had never excited her the way this hard, unknowable man did?

She gathered her breath as they finally reached his suite. He released her hand to open the door, then stood on the threshold, his large frame even more imposing in the moonlight.

She should make her excuses and leave.

She'd always been impulsive, but what was she doing, allowing Kamal Zokan to drag her to his room like a possession?

What are you doing, Liah? However exciting he is, even you can't be this reckless!

But, as she tried to think of a diplomatic way out, the silence pressed in upon her, trapping the words in her throat behind the great big ball of reckless lust and intoxicating energy.

Her body didn't feel like her own any more. She felt enthralled, spellbound, driven to do dangerous things. And it was intoxicating. He hadn't said a word ever since they had left the reception. But then, she hadn't really expected him to. Even from their brief acquaintance, she already knew he was a man who preferred action to words.

'If you have changed your mind, I will escort you back to the reception,' he said at last.

She should be relieved. But something about the fact he had sensed her indecision—when she would never have suspected he had a sensitive bone in his body—called to the reckless gene that had made her do stupid things her entire life.

Especially when his expression, so full of hunger moments before, became shuttered and a cynical smile tilted his lips.

'After all, I cannot offer you more than one night,' he added.

The words—so arrogant, so full of amused indifference—called to that rebellious streak like a red rag waved before a charging bull.

He was expecting her to chicken out.

The bastard.

The hot, fluid throb of arousal was joined by the fierce pulse of adrenaline.

'What makes you think I *want* more than one night?' she shot back.

Why was she fighting this need, this hunger?

Something about this man made her want him more than she had ever wanted any other man. But surely this was just chemistry, pheromones? Maybe it didn't even have that much to do with him. Maybe it was merely the frustration of Colin's cruel betrayal finally coming home to roost. She wasn't frigid, and now she would prove it.

One night would suit her just fine. She wanted to know what it felt like to have wild, untamed, no-holds-barred sex with a man who wanted the same thing. And nothing more. There could never be more between them. Their pasts, their futures, their goals, desires and ambitions could not be more different.

A man like Prince Kamal would never touch her heart.

'Because you are a woman, and sometimes a woman cannot tell the difference between sex and emotion,' he supplied, clearly not realising her question had been rhetorical.

Liah gasped, momentarily speechless.

Of all the chauvinistic…!

The adrenaline surged. She grabbed his lapels and yanked his face down to hers, determined to show him who was boss.

'It's lucky I'm not your average woman, then,' she snapped.

The fierce, unfettered need in his gaze turned the deep amber to a fiery gold. 'Good,' he replied.

Then his lips slanted across hers in a shockingly possessive kiss. Need fired through her system as his tongue drove into her mouth, demanding entry. Her lips opened for him, instinctively, need throbbing into erogenous zones she'd never realised she had as he feasted on her as if he owned her.

His hands roamed over her naked back where the gown plunged and he tugged her into his body. The solid, unyielding strength of him made her writhe against him, the riot of sensations too fierce, too full.

She heard her own sharp intake of breath as he explored the recesses of her mouth, commanding, devastating, as the pulsing sensation centred at her core. The weight that had tormented her all night became jammed between her thighs, growing to impossible proportions and making the ache painful—even as she kissed him back with equal fervour.

He ripped his mouth away, his large, callused palms rising to grasp her cheeks, to angle her head for better access, then he sunk into her again.

Their tongues tangled in a battle of need and desire, as much argument as acquiescence, each trying to gain the upper hand.

When they were finally forced to part again, to catch

their breaths, she could feel the thick ridge of his erection pressing into her belly.

'Be aware, no matter how good this is, it can only be for tonight,' he rasped, his hand resting on her cheek as he brushed the curls behind her ear. 'I cannot commit to more.'

The arrogant jerk.

'Well, then, it's good I'm only interested in you for your body, pal,' she shot back, determined to prove she would never mistake endorphins for love.

Instead of being offended as she had intended, though, he simply laughed, the rumbling chuckle gruff with approval.

'Yes, it will be very good,' he replied. Before she could get even more indignant, he scooped her up into his arms and strode into the suite.

He carried her through the living area into the master bedroom. A full moon gave the lavish Moorish furnishings a luminous glow. Her breathing accelerated as he set her down beside the huge king-size bed. With its colourful silk cushions piled high on one end, and the intricate screens that shielded them from the night gilded by moonlight, the setting seemed fanciful and romantic.

She gulped down a ragged breath.

Not romantic. This was a transaction of passion— nothing more, nothing less.

But as he turned her body towards the open terrace doors, then unpicked the jewelled pins from her hair before drawing the heavy mass to one side and kissing her nape, his callused hands almost reverent, her breath got trapped in her lungs.

She could see the gardens below the balcony. Fountains and exotic plants made the space an enchanted oasis—or so she'd dreamed as a child while she'd roamed the palace grounds with her brother William, pretending to be a fairy queen. The dim lights of the old women's quarters in the distance and the dark windows of her family's private suites on the opposite terrace, where her two younger brothers were probably asleep, made something hard and scary lodge in her gut. What had happened to those long-ago dreams of finding love and romance she'd once had within these walls—a passion for the ages, like the one her parents shared?

The sudden fear that the step she was taking tonight wasn't as small or insignificant as she wanted it to be assailed her as Kamal's lips left her neck and she heard him take off his jacket and dump it on the chair beside her.

You're not a little girl any more, and you haven't been for a while. It's past time to become a woman.

His thumb rubbed against the hammering pulse at her collarbone. 'Is there a problem?'

She jolted at the gruff and far too perceptive question.

Could he sense her hesitation, her fear? Not of him, but of what this night might mean, even though she didn't want it to mean anything other than a chance to finally find out what all the fuss was about.

She spun round—to find him watching her with the

hunger undimmed in his eyes, an unreadable expression on his face.

He was so close. He'd not only lost the jacket but the bow-tie too and had unbuttoned the confining collar she knew he hated while she had been taking her daft trip down memory lane. His thick hair stuck up in haphazard rows, as if he'd run impatient fingers through it while she'd stood and romanticised this moment like a fool.

A new layer of stubble had grown over his jaw in just a few hours, making him look like a pirate or a bandit. But it was the gleam in his eyes that seemed to yank at her heart and sink deep into her abdomen—compelling, exciting, dangerous.

'There's no problem,' she said, determined to believe it.

This was just a virgin's jitters.

'You are sure?' he said, his voice so low she could barely hear it.

'Yes, absolutely,' she replied with a certainty she didn't feel but was determined to make herself believe.

This was just sex, not a relationship. She didn't have to care about the fairy tales she'd made up as a little girl in the enchanted garden below them.

And she certainly didn't have to imagine the man she had envisioned falling in love with one day—a man who would be strong but tender, fiercely intelligent, commanding and determined, but also kind and patient. Because Prince Kamal was not that man, nor would he ever be.

The only thing that mattered now was tonight.

She stretched on tiptoes to unbutton his shirt the rest of the way. Her fingers trembled, her movements frantic and clumsy. But, as she finally reached the bottom and tugged the cotton out of his cummerbund to reveal the ridges of his six-pack, his large hand captured her fingers, preventing her from caressing the golden skin.

Her head jerked up, panic joining the fierce need.

'What?' she asked, scared he was going to stop her. Had he guessed how inexperienced she was?

He tugged her fingers to his lips and kissed the tips. The gesture was almost tender, until he sucked one finger into his mouth, and what had been strangely sweet became devastatingly erotic, the drawing sensation echoing painfully in her sex.

At last he released her hand to lift her hair from her neck and press those marauding lips to the pulse at her throat. He licked and suckled, sending brutal sensation pounding down.

'There is no rush,' he whispered with gruff amusement. 'We have all night.'

Was he laughing at her? She wanted to be indignant, annoyed. But it was hard to be anything but desperate when with deliberate purpose he parted the plunging V of her gown's neckline to reveal her breasts to his burning gaze.

His brow furrowed as he skimmed a thumb under the swollen flesh. 'What is this?'

She glanced down and realised the problem—the flesh-coloured discs which covered her breasts, making them look weird. Heat mottled the skin across her collarbone.

'Um, my bra. It's a stick-on.'

'Ingenious,' he murmured as he circled the rubberised discs. 'Does it hurt to remove them?'

She huffed out a strained laugh. *Awkward, much?* 'No.'

He brushed his thumb across the peak of her breast, the nipple distending beneath its shield.

She sucked in a breath. She could see his amusement, but also the fierce passion that hadn't dimmed.

'May I remove them?' he asked.

Speech deserted her at the bold request. She'd never quite envisioned her first seduction being this awkward, or this hot.

'Yes,' she managed.

To her astonishment, he sunk to his knees which, because of his height, brought his head level with her breasts. For several pregnant seconds, he studied the design. Then he slipped his fingernail under the gel-like substance and peeled it back with infinite care.

She grasped his broad shoulders, the prickling sensation made unbearably erotic by his concentration. His wide shoulders bunched beneath the shirt, but then he threw away the stick-on and licked across the nipple.

The rush of feeling as the tip engorged was like nothing she had ever felt before. The nipple, already tender, swelled and throbbed as he lathed the peak, his large hands capturing her hips to hold her steady for the delicious torment.

A cool breeze brushed across her tender flesh as he leaned back on his heels then proceeded to peel away the other bra cup. Again, he played with the exposed nipple with his tongue, making darts of brutal sensation arrow into her sex. At last, he captured the swollen peak between his lips and suckled hard.

Her body bowed forward, her fingers sinking into his hair as heady, insistent desire fanned out from her breast and blazed a trail through all her erogenous zones.

She was weak, panting, barely able to stand, when he finally released her from the exquisite torture. He stood to ease the gown over her hips until she was standing before him in nothing more than her lacy thong.

She folded an arm across her breasts, every one of her senses heightened, aware of the slick moisture dampening her panties.

'Do not hide yourself from me,' he said, the comment part-request but mostly demand. To her surprise, she released her arm on his command.

Her back arched as she lifted her breasts. She wanted him to see all of her. Wanted to experience the rush of exhilaration as he thumbed the nipple, his breath gushing out on a grunt of need.

'It's your turn,' she managed, suddenly desperate to see him too, to touch, tempt and devour him the way he had done to her.

His head lifted, but then he lowered it to concentrate on unzipping his trousers.

Power surged through her and she had the strangest sense of a man, who took orders from no one, taking orders from her.

He kicked off his shoes and dragged off his trousers and boxer shorts together.

Suddenly he stood before her, naked except for the open shirt that he hadn't removed. She wanted to demand he lose that too, but all she could do was shiver uncontrollably as she devoured the sight of him—magnificent and strange, his big, perfectly formed body gilded by moonlight. Dark curls of hair bloomed around his nipples, defining the heavy slabs of his pectoral muscles, then trailed into a thin line to bisect his abdominal muscles. His obliques stood out, arrowing down to his groin, and the bush of dark hair did nothing to disguise the thrusting erection.

She drew in a staggered breath, feeling light-headed. *Oh. My.*

The column of his sex stood upright, bending towards his belly button. She'd never seen a man's naked penis before, and certainly not one so magnificently erect, but she was sure very few could compare to the length and girth of this one.

Her throat dried, even as the moisture flooded between her thighs. She should have been panicked—how on earth was all of that going to fit inside her?—but somehow all she felt was a heady charge at the sight of him, so hard, so ready, just for her.

'Can I…can I touch it?' she stammered, her voice low with awe.

His eyebrows shot up his forehead and then he laughed. 'Of course,' he said, his tone more than a little incredulous.

Humiliation flared and she wanted to bite off her own tongue.

Way to go, Liah—why not make it totally obvious you're a virgin?

As if she needed to make him any more big-headed. She swallowed down the pulse of embarrassment.

It doesn't matter what he thinks...you will never see him again after tonight.

Reaching out, she traced her fingertip down the thick length.

He groaned as the long column seemed to bend to her touch. Heat scoured her insides, but this time it had nothing to do with mortification and everything to do with excitement. She wrapped her fingers around him, marvelling at the way the flesh felt so soft and yet so solid. His breathing accelerated, and his abdominal muscles tensed as he stood, stoic and unmoving, and let her explore.

A bead of moisture appeared at the tip, fascinating her even more. She rubbed her thumb across the straining head, using the viscous liquid to ease her grip as she stroked the velvet length.

He made a guttural sound. The power surged as he swelled and throbbed in her hand.

But, just as the empty ache in her core became unbearable, her need reaching fever pitch at the thought of seeing him lose control, he grasped her wrist and pulled her fingers away.

'Enough,' he murmured, his tone no longer mocking. 'Do you wish to unman me?' he asked, the question raw.

She smiled. 'Yes?'

He laughed. The rough chuckle was like a balm to her soul. Her heart swelled at the weird, disconnected thought that, for all his arrogance and even chauvinism, this man had no problem seeing her as an equal. He enjoyed the challenge, the battle for supremacy between them, as much as she did. He didn't think less of her for wanting to best him, he actually thought more.

But, before she had a chance to contemplate that bizarre revelation—which surely had to be the endorphins talking?—he scooped her into his arms again to carry her to the bed.

He tossed her onto the wide mattress as if she weighed nothing.

'You little witch,' he murmured as he joined her on the bed, his big body looming over hers. 'Two can play at that game.'

She scrambled backwards, but he grasped her ankle to draw her towards him. Cradling her hips, he knelt between her legs then cupped her bottom to bring her throbbing centre towards his marauding mouth.

She squirmed, as shocked as she was exhilarated. Was he actually going to kiss her…*there*…?

He parted her folds with his thumbs then blew softly across the heated flesh, which did nothing whatsoever to cool the vicious heat.

'Yes… Please.' She didn't even recognise the guttural plea as her own until her gaze met the vivid amber of his eyes, the wicked intent in them as intoxicating as the desperate need making her pulse points throb and the slick flesh between her legs swell.

He breathed in, then groaned. 'You smell so delicious. I may have to feast on you all night.'

He was teasing her, but the playful words seemed part-promise, part-threat.

Before she could come up with a counter claim, he licked across the swollen folds. Her hips bucked involuntarily, almost throwing him off, the sensation so raw, so real, her whole body seemed concentrated on that one melting spot.

He held her firmly and continued to probe and swirl, finding the very heart of her desire and ruthlessly exploiting it. She sobbed, the sounds crude and elemental as she sank back on the bed and gave herself over to the brutal passion, the devastating need.

The coil tightened like a vice, her body becoming one raw, throbbing bundle of sensation centred on the devastating play of his tongue as she bucked and writhed against his hold.

Then he captured the swollen nub at last and suckled hard.

The vicious climax slammed into her, bursting into a thousand glittering shards. She came down slowly, aware of him licking her through the last of the brutal orgasm, her body shuddering in the wake of something so shattering, she wasn't sure she would ever feel her extremities again.

'Please, I can't...' She touched his hair and felt the silken waves beneath her fingers.

He stopped abruptly and rose above her.

She watched in a daze, her mind blown, as he leaned

over her and produced a small foil packet from the bedside table.

He rolled it on the thick erection, so distended now it looked even more overwhelming than it had before. But somehow the sight only made the empty ache at her core more desperate to be filled.

He cradled her hips in shaky palms. The spurt of power, at the knowledge he wasn't as steady or controlled as he appeared, was a welcome relief. Maybe she had lost the battle, but she had not lost the war. Yet.

He probed, finding the slick heart of her, then pressed forward in one smooth, devastating thrust.

She gasped and flinched, gripping the hard muscles of his shoulders under his shirt. He felt immense between her legs, the pulse of pleasure dimming to become sharp and discordant.

He stopped abruptly, holding still inside her. 'Are you all right? You are very tight,' he added, the concern in his voice calling to a place deep inside her.

She shook her head, the pain easing as she adjusted to his size.

'No, don't stop,' she said, surprising herself a little. She didn't want him to stop. Didn't want him to withdraw. Yes, he was overwhelming, but the pleasure was already returning, sensation building—her body eager to endure anything to enjoy another shattering release.

Her fingers glided over his shoulders, feeling strange ridges…what were those?…as she loosened her grip to let him sink the rest of the way into her.

'I want all of you,' she murmured in the darkness.

The words should have been merely sexual, but he

jolted, and something flickered into his eyes—something surprised but also wary.

He eased out, then pressed back. She groaned as he rolled his hips, easing the tight, stretched feeling by incremental degrees.

The pleasure rippled, sparkled, bubbling up from her centre again.

'Good?' he asked.

'Yes, very good,' she said, and he groaned.

At last, he was buried inside her to the hilt. Raw emotion blindsided her at how gentle, how careful, he had been. The exquisite pleasure pulsed as her body tightened around his, massaging his thick length. She doubted she would orgasm like this but, even as she resigned herself, he pulled out to thrust back, adjusting the angle.

Shocking sensation rolled through her as he rubbed a spot she hadn't known existed. She sobbed, the desperate sound echoing around the room. The pleasure built again, so raw, so elemental, too much and not enough, as his movements became more forceful, more demanding. Her hands slipped on his sweat-slicked shoulders, feeling those confusing ridges again as she braced for the ruthlessly deep stroking, each thrust taking her higher, further, but never quite taking her over.

She clung to him, aware of every sight, every sound, every sensation, and aware of nothing except the power of his body and that deep, internal caress swelling the wave of release.

Suddenly he took one hand from her hip and delved

where their bodies joined, rubbing his thumb over her clitoris.

'Come for me now, Kaliah,' he ordered.

The cataclysmic wave crashed over her at last, as if at his command.

He stiffened above her, his shout of fulfilment matching her fierce cries. The wave swept her over that high wide peak until she found herself tumbling into a hot vat of stunning pleasure, impossible bliss. Her heart hammered her chest wall so hard, she was surprised he couldn't feel it as he dropped on top of her, following her into the bottomless abyss.

She clasped him to her breast, blinking back tears as stunning afterglow enveloped her.

She could feel his heart beating for several precious, beautiful moments as she absorbed the shocking intensity of their joining. And it occurred to her that for all his flaws—and she was sure she didn't even know the half of them—Kamal Zokan had made her first time magnificent.

But then he lifted off her, withdrawing slowly as she released him with difficulty.

He rolled away from her onto his back. 'That was good, yes?' he said.

'Yes,' she replied, stupidly touched he would ask.

Get a grip, Liah. It's just sex, remember? Sex and chemistry. Really spectacular chemistry.

Which had to be why she couldn't stem the surge of joy and gratitude making her throat close and her heart hurt.

His large hand landed on her thigh, his thumb caressing the bare skin in a lazily possessive manner that only made her heart thunder harder.

A renewed jolt of pleasure shot through her exhausted flesh, despite the soreness at her core.

Down, girl.

She shifted, ready to pull away from his touch. But then he rolled towards her and tucked her body into the lee of his. She could feel the thick length, still semi-firm, pressed into her bottom. His breathing slowed to an even rhythm as his arms wrapped around her waist.

Her heart jolted and swelled, disturbing her even more.

Prince Kamal's a snuggler... Who would have guessed?

'Sleep now.' His deep voice rumbled against her back. 'Then we can go again when I am recovered.'

Her heart jolted. But, instead of feeling indignant at his arrogance, and the assumption she would stay in his arms all night without being asked, all she felt was the stupid pulse of gratitude that he would want her.

His breathing deepened behind her, his arm becoming heavier as he relaxed into sleep.

She lay staring at the full moon through the latticed window, breathing in the potent perfume of night jasmine from the garden below—which had enchanted her as a girl and flavoured all those foolish dreams—and tried to gather her shattered wits. But the perfume of the night garden was masked by the even more compelling scent of sex, sweat and him.

She forced herself to ignore the painful squeeze in her ribs as she became aware of the soreness between her legs. She couldn't stay, and certainly didn't want to risk another session or she might mistake the pain in her ribs for something other than endorphins.

But, even so, when she finally managed to tug herself out of his arms she couldn't quite make herself believe that what had happened between them meant nothing.

She dressed furtively in the moonlight, then rushed through the shadowy palace corridors back to the safety of her own rooms, while the ache in her chest refused to ease.

And as she washed the scent of him from her body, far too aware of all the places where he had touched and caressed her, she couldn't seem to wash away the fear she had lost an important part of herself.

CHAPTER FOUR

LIAH WOKE AS the knocking in her head became real.

She groaned, every single spot Kamal had explored last night aching in unison.

'Who is it?' she shouted. And what time was it? Because bright daylight was shining through the screen on her terrace.

Damn, she must have over-slept. A lot.

'It is Aisha, Highness,' came the reply, from one of her mother's private secretaries. 'Their Majesties ask that you join them in the Sheikh's private study as soon as possible.'

That was weird—she only ever got called to her dad's study on official business or when she'd screwed up.

'Okay, do you know what this is about?' Liah asked, sitting up and clasping her sheet to her tender breasts as Aisha popped her head around the bed-chamber door.

'I am not at liberty to say, Your Highness,' the usually level-headed woman said as she flushed a deep red. 'But they require your presence as soon as possible…'

Heat burned in Liah's cheeks. Had her parents spotted Kamal and her high-tailing it out of the reception last night?

Even as the mortification threatened to engulf her, she dismissed the idea. This was just her guilty conscience talking, because she'd left his room last night without saying goodbye.

She was a grown woman. While her father might dress her down for risking her neck on what he thought was an untrained horse, her parents would never judge her for her personal choices.

Even so, the heated blush refused to subside.

After Aisha had disappeared, Liah flung off the sheet and shot across the room, ignoring the discomfort between her thighs. Whatever this was about, she needed to get it out the way before she could flee to the Aleaza Oasis, the special place where she always went when she needed a time-out from palace life.

Not *flee*, she corrected herself, locating an outfit while simultaneously trying to tame her epic bed-hair. She wasn't fleeing the palace, or Prince Kamal. She was simply taking a break for three days, while her one-night lover returned to his own kingdom, so she could lock the disturbing intimacy they had shared last night into a box marked 'no biggie'.

Twenty minutes later, as she tapped on her father's study door, she was still struggling to get the stupid blush under control.

'Come in, Liah,' her father called.

Stepping into the room, she spotted her father seated

at his desk and her mother standing behind him, her vivid chestnut eyes rich with...*what was that?*

Because her mother was wearing the sort of concerned expression Liah remembered from her childhood, when she'd done something reckless, or dangerous...or both.

Her gaze darted to her dad. But he didn't look mad, he looked concerned too.

'Liah, sit down. We have a situation we need to discuss,' her father said, his voice so grave she began to panic.

But then another far too familiar voice rumbled from behind her. 'There is no discussion necessary, Your Majesty. We must be married. The Crown Princess was a virgin when we slept together last night. It is the honourable course, and also the responsibility of every sheikh, to offer marriage to any woman whose virginity he takes. Is this not written in the Law of Marriage of the Sheikhs?'

The humiliating blush napalmed Liah's cheeks as she swung round and her horrified gaze landed on the man she hadn't spotted sitting behind the door.

His tall, indomitable frame rose like a phoenix from the ashes of her memory—or more like a dragon from its lair—incinerating the last of her composure in the process as he strode towards her.

Conflicting emotions charged through her system at warp speed—shock, embarrassment, mortification—but worse was the wave of something rich and fluid as all the sore, tender spots began to throb.

But then she registered his grim expression. He

looked even less pleased to see her than she was to see him—which, on the scale of not being pleased was on a par with getting kicked in the gut by Ashreen. Then his outrageous proposal registered and the choking rage rose up her throat like acid.

He'd told her parents about their one-night stand—their *private, secret, never-to-be-repeated* one-night stand—and the fact she had been a virgin… And now he expected her to *marry* him because of some arcane law.

She spluttered. The only thing shocking her more than Kamal's unbelievable gall was the fact her head hadn't exploded.

Then the outrage spewed out of her mouth, like lava erupting from a volcano.

'Are you completely and utterly nuts?'

Kamal clenched his fists so hard, he could feel his fingernails cutting into his palms as he battled the desire to grab the infuriating woman in front of him and throw her over his lap so he could give her the spanking she so richly deserved.

He had never laid a hand on a woman without her consent in his entire life—and certainly not in anger—but right now he could feel every fibre of his being straining to maintain the cast-iron control he had acquired, after a childhood of abuse and an adulthood of having every one of his desires and ambitions questioned and judged.

He would not lose his temper, or his civility. But it was a hard-fought battle. Harder than any of the many others he had fought in his twenty-nine years. She had left him in the night, without a word, like a thief. But, worse, she had not told him of her virgin state.

'Do you deny I am your first lover?' he asked, to be absolutely sure he had not jumped to the wrong conclusion when he had awoken, heavily erect and aching to sink inside her again, to find the bed beside him empty and speckles of blood on the sheets, probably evidence of her virgin state.

The vivid blush on her face darkened and her breasts rose and fell beneath the fitted T-shirt she wore with jeans and boots which displayed her slender frame far too effectively.

'That is absolutely none of your business,' she said.

Which was not a denial.

He was right—she *had* been a virgin—which meant she had put them both in an impossible position for which there was only one solution. This wayward, reckless, infuriating woman would have to become his wife.

His honour demanded it, as a man and a prince. And so did hers as a member of Narabia's royal family.

The Law of Marriage of the Sheikhs was an important responsibility for every ruling male in all the kingdoms of the region. If a man in his position took a woman's virginity, he was compelled to offer marriage. He had been taught as much during the lessons on Zokari cultural traditions and institutions he had been required to take to prepare him for the throne.

Kamal's eyes narrowed. 'Do you think the Law of Marriage does not apply to me because I was not born of royal blood?' he sneered, his anger starting to strangle him.

Was that it? Had she believed she could deceive him about her virgin state because he had no right to his throne?

'*What?* No, of course not.' Her eyebrows lifted, the blush becoming radioactive. 'I just don't give a toss about such a stupid, archaic tradition.'

'You think tradition and culture is stupid?' He raised his voice, the desire to spank her so all-consuming now, his palms began to itch. 'You dishonour your family, your country and yourself with this attitude, and you also dishonour me. You will become my wife now or—'

'There's no way on Earth I would become your wife under any circumstances,' she interrupted him. *Again*. 'You're an arrogant, overbearing—'

'Okay, *enough*!' The shout from her father had them both turning to see the Sheikh stand and stride around his desk. 'Stop yelling, the both of you, and sit down.'

Kamal straightened, having completely forgotten Sheikh Zane Ali and his wife were in the room the minute their wayward daughter had appeared.

But the brief spurt of shame was swiftly quashed. This situation was not of his making, and he refused to be placated or dismissed by anyone. Not even a man as powerful and well-respected as the Narabian Sheikh. He might be embarrassed the man and his wife had witnessed their unseemly spat, but he planned to marry their daughter and they would have to get used to it, as well as her.

He had requested a meeting with the Sheikh this morning and had told him of last night's development—after finally getting over his own fury with the shoddy way Kaliah Khan had treated him, enough to think coherently, at least. When he had formally requested the man's daughter's hand in marriage, Zane Khan had not reacted the way he had expected.

Instead of seeing marriage as the only solution, he had seemed circumspect, and had insisted on calling in the Crown Princess to 'discuss' the situation. There was no discussion Kamal could imagine that would change the facts, and he did not like the way the man was looking at them both now, as if this was some kind of lovers' quarrel which needed to be handled instead of an extremely damaging diplomatic incident.

He took a moment to breathe through his anger—which meant keeping his eyes off the woman beside him and focussing on her father.

He did not take orders from Zane Khan or any man, and he would not be thwarted on this. But, at the same time, he was in the man's home. And he did not wish to make an enemy of Khan, or risk him withdrawing his endorsement, not unless he absolutely had to.

'I will not sit until we have an agreement on this,' he said, deliberately leaving off the honorific.

'If you think you're getting me to agree to marry you…' Kaliah began, but her father simply lifted his hand.

'Liah, just sit down, damn it,' he said, weary resignation in his voice. 'And stop making things worse.'

'But, Dad, you can't be seriously entertaining any of this?' she said, a high, desperate note entering her voice.

Kamal stared at them both, confused by the familiarity with which she addressed her father. He had noticed it before, after the race, and he couldn't help but be astonished by it.

He had no understanding of how families worked, having never had one of his own, but surely it could not be right that she would talk to her Sheikh with such disrespect? Although, somehow, Kaliah Khan's wilful behaviour did not surprise him. It seemed the woman had no respect for anything—not the culture and traditions which had bound their region for centuries, and certainly not him or the gravity of what they had shared the previous night.

Her audacious behaviour only annoyed him more. Did she actually believe he *wanted* to marry her? As much as he might need a wife, and as much as he had enjoyed the sex, he was not a fool. Their chemistry was explosive, that was certainly true. But the intensity of their physical connection had also disturbed him. The fact he'd been her first only disturbed him more.

How could she have been so enchanting, so alluring? How could his climax have been so…he breathed, trying to prevent the bolt of desire journeying any further south…overwhelming when she had been so inexperienced? How could she have had him clinging to his control? And where had that damned possessive streak come from, which had blindsided him as soon as he'd seen the flecks of blood?

He was good at sex. He had learned how to pleasure women as a young soldier. Pasha—his first lover—had been in her thirties and a widow. She had been patient and kind with him and had taught him well. And, until last night, he had always enjoyed using his skill to bring a woman to orgasm before he found his own release.

But, with Kaliah Khan, patient enjoyment had become desperate need. It had almost killed him to hold back. If he had interpreted her odd mix of boldness and shyness for what it was last night, he would have stopped before it was too late if she'd asked him to. But seeing her again, feeling the vicious surge of desire all over again, only made him realise how hard that would have been…when it should have been easy.

How could he still want her so desperately? Enough even to want to marry her on one level, although he knew she was the precise opposite of the sort of woman he should make his queen.

He needed a partner, a woman who could respect him and look up to him—despite his past—a woman who was mature, responsible and most of all willing to listen and learn. And it was clear, from this morning's display of hubris, entitlement and reckless disregard for everything except herself, that Kaliah Khan was not that woman.

'Please, Prince Kamal, perhaps if you sit down… if you *both* sit down…' the Queen said, sending her daughter a pointed look, 'We could all discuss this like rational adults.'

He frowned. Was Queen Catherine implying *he* was

not behaving like an adult? Before his temper could spike again, though, he registered the beseeching look in the older woman's warm chestnut eyes and his temper defused a little...

He forced himself to walk stiffly back to his chair and sit down. He waited, aware of Kaliah's rigid stance, the temper bristling off her as she continued to stand and glare at both her parents. He felt an odd ripple of sympathy. Apparently, she did not enjoy being trapped any more than he did. Even if it was all her own fault.

At last, she trudged over to the chair opposite her father's desk—the chair furthest from his own, he noted—and sat. He ignored her petty show of defiance.

Her desires made no difference now. Surely she would have to bend to her father's will and honour the traditions she had been born into, whether she wished it or not? They both would.

Her father returned to his desk and sat behind it. Steepling his fingers, he directed his gaze at his daughter and asked quietly, 'Is it true, Liah? Did you sleep with Prince Kamal last night and were you a virgin?'

'Dad!' Kaliah leapt back out of her chair. 'You're not seriously asking me that question?' she cried. 'What I do in my private life is none of...'

Khan put up a placating hand to interrupt her latest disrespectful diatribe. 'Okay, okay, Liah. Calm down. I'm just trying to establish the facts, that's all.'

It was obvious from the pained look on the Sheikh's face, though, that he knew what Kamal had told him was the truth, because his daughter had yet to deny it.

Kamal sat rigidly in his chair, ignoring the confusion and the fury bubbling like acid under his breast-bone. Not to mention the low-grade arousal that was always there when he was within two feet of Zane Khan's unruly daughter.

He waited for Khan to state the obvious—that a marriage would have to be arranged—but, instead of doing so, Khan turned to Kamal, his expression strained but resolute.

Kamal didn't like that look one bit because he had seen it many times before. In the face of Uttram Aziz when he had announced Kamal would have to marry to secure the throne. In the face of his commanding officer, during his first desert campaign, when he had been ordered to take his troops into bandit country with no cover, and only himself and four of his men had come out alive. In the face of Hamid, when his employer had unwound his belt to give him another brutal beating—unlike the staff at the orphanage, or his first drill sergeant when he had entered the Zokari army, Hamid had been a bully who'd enjoyed exploiting the power he'd held over that defenceless boy.

He also remembered that look from his earliest memory—when a tall man had told him to be a good boy then walked away, leaving him on the steps of the orphanage. He hated that look because he knew it meant only one thing—he was about to get shafted.

'Here's the thing, Prince Kamal,' the Sheikh said with an apologetic note in his voice, despite the determination in his eyes. 'While the Law of Marriage of the Sheikhs is an honourable tradition, meant to protect women—and I can totally understand why you, as a conscientious and clearly honourable man, would want to adhere to it—in Narabia it's not something we would insist upon any more, unless both parties are one hundred percent amenable.'

Kamal's anger rose in his chest, but he kept his gaze on Khan and refused to let any of the emotions churning in his gut—everything from indignation to fury—show. Because that would just give this man the upper hand.

'What does this mean, exactly?' he asked, determined to make Khan spell it out.

'That you have no obligation to marry my daughter just because you took her virginity last night,' he said. 'It's fairly clear from what my wife and I have just witnessed that there's no love lost between the two of you,' the man continued, the tinge of paternal condescension making the fire in Kamal's gut burn. 'And I very much doubt you wish to be shackled to Liah any more than she wishes to be shackled to you.'

'Gee, thanks, Dad,' Kaliah muttered, but Kamal could hear the relief in her tone and wanted to punch a wall.

They were telling him his honour, his country's honour, did not matter. And he could not accept that. But, worse, they were suggesting the responsibility he now felt for Kaliah was of no significance too.

Khan let out a deep sigh, then grasped the hand his wife had laid on his shoulder while he'd spoken.

Something about that gesture, the visceral connection between this man and his wife—supportive, generous and fierce—only made Kamal feel more alone. And more isolated.

The fire leapt in his gut. Damn them. He didn't need anyone's support. He had always survived on his own.

'So, basically, I think we can all just pretend this never happened. And the details of last night's…' Khan cleared his throat uncomfortably '…last night's events will never leave this room, so no one's honour need be challenged. You've fulfilled your obligation by coming here and proposing, Kamal, and I appreciate it. But I'm not about to require you to marry a woman you don't love,' he finished.

Love? What on earth was the man talking about? An emotion as fickle, fanciful and foolish as love had no bearing on any of this. And Kamal certainly did not require love. Not from anyone. He never had and he never would. He had himself—that was all he required.

'I hope you will stay for the rest of the weekend?' Khan added. 'As our honoured guest.'

Kamal had no intention of staying after being insulted so comprehensively. But he needed time to think before he made his next move. He had come to Khan this morning expecting this to be fairly straightforward. Clearly the man was even more indulgent of his wayward daughter than Kamal had realised. But he would find a solution once he could unknot his brain enough to think clearly.

'As you wish.' Kamal stood, too furious to say more or even to look at the woman who was the cause of this disaster. His pride was burning, but what was far worse was the way the pain in his gut had morphed into the gruelling hollow ache he remembered so well from much of his adolescence—every time he'd faced another rejection, another put down, another cruel dismissal, because he'd never been strong enough, never brave enough, never important enough to matter.

He gave a shallow bow and strode out of the room.

He was not that sad, rejected boy any longer.

And he would prove it by showing Kaliah Khan that Crown Prince Kamal Zokan was good enough for any woman. And certainly one as wild, spoilt and wilful as Narabia's future queen.

CHAPTER FIVE

LIAH SWIPED THE angry tear from her cheek as she spurred Ashreen over the rocky escarpment. She glanced over her shoulder in the gathering dusk. The minarets of the Golden Palace had disappeared behind the mountain ridge.

The crushing weight that had been sitting on her chest ever since she had been ambushed by Prince Kamal in her father's study finally lifted a little. But, as she tugged on the reins to slow Ashreen before they headed down the rocky slope to the oasis, the knots in her gut refused to ease.

She'd never been more humiliated in her whole entire life than she had been that morning. And that was saying something for someone who seemed so adept at screwing up on a regular basis.

She'd trudged back to her room, packed a small bag and had waited—while regretting every single wrong, foolish decision that had led to the worse mistake she'd ever made last night by deciding to sleep with that man. No one had come to ask her to attend any of the day's events, and she knew why. She suspected her parents were keen to keep her away from Kamal—and stave off a diplomatic incident.

As soon as the sun had dipped towards the horizon, making the weather cool enough to ride out to the oasis, she had sneaked down to the stables, saddled Ashreen and escaped, leaving a note with one of the stable hands to deliver to Malik, her father's head of household. She didn't want her parents to worry, but at the same time she very much doubted they'd be sad to see the back of her right now.

Another tear leaked out. She pushed it away, knowing she had no right to be upset. These were tears of self-pity.

Why can't you ever get any single thing right?

She tried to re-gather some of her anger towards Kamal and his outrageous demands, which had managed to sustain at least a little of her pride and self-worth during that awful meeting. But the scalding anger had died hours ago…and all she felt towards him now was a vague feeling of misery.

Because she couldn't get the image out of her head of his face as her father had informed him there would be no marriage. For once he had been completely transparent. And, while the foremost emotion had definitely been fury, what she'd also seen was confusion and something that had looked uncomfortably like shame.

As much as she wanted to hate him, she could see she was the one who had been thoughtless and selfish. She'd used him to lose her virginity.

She flushed as the memory of his lips, his tongue and his teeth on her flowed through her again. She could still feel the slow glide of his callused palms owning every inch of her body, making her beg and moan, setting off fires that had finally overwhelmed her completely when his hard, thick length had pressed relentlessly but so carefully into her tender flesh. And she'd surrendered the last of herself to him.

Heat pulsed and throbbed in the sore spots that still troubled her after last night. Why hadn't it even occurred to her that there would be emotional repercussions, not just for her, but for him too?

The truth was, she'd totally forgotten about that silly old law, but why hadn't she figured out that Kamal would consider taking her virginity something he would have to atone for?

On one level, the whole concept of him insisting on marriage was totally nuts. But she knew nothing about him—how he'd come to the throne, the mysterious 'background' her father had alluded to—and she hadn't bothered to ask.

Typical Liah. Just dive in head-first, do what feels good and don't bother considering anyone else's feelings or responsibilities.

Shame flooded through her as she spotted the oasis in the distance.

The iridescent pool of water, fed by a spring that flowed over limestone rocks, shimmered in the twilight as night fell. The grove of palms, shrubs and desert blooms provided much-needed shade from the bitter desert sun in the day time. The luxury encampment—several tents and a corral—was kept well-stocked and regularly checked by her father's staff to ensure her family could escape here when necessary. And it was also a good bolt hole for unwary travellers who got lost in the regions vast and unforgiving landscape.

As she released her hold on Ashreen, the horse broke into a canter, having scented the fresh water. But somehow the place which had always fortified and liberated her as a teenager, a place where she knew she could be one hundred percent herself, felt less of a well-earned escape this evening…and more like a coward's hideout. Even this oasis couldn't change the fact she would never be the woman her family needed her to be.

Not a queen. Not a mature woman. But a spoilt child.

After dismounting, she tugged off the saddle and the rest of the tack, her arms aching. As she rubbed the horse down, and fed and watered her before attending to her own needs, she tried to rationalise away the weight still crushing her ribs.

She hadn't slept well last night. Maybe she just needed a few days here to get over this feeling of ennui and hopelessness? Once Kamal left the palace and returned to Zokar, she would surely be able to make amends for her latest disaster?

But the memory of the disappointment in both her parents' faces made her stomach tangle into a tight knot of regret. Far worse, though, was the memory of the look in Kamal Zokan's eyes when he'd walked out of her father's study—angry and intense but also guarded and wary and, for a moment, beaten down.

Way to go, Liah. The undisputed Queen of Monumental Screw-Ups.

After she had bathed off the trail dust in the cool spring water and lit the torches to keep any unwanted visitors away, she collapsed into the tent and stared at the sturdy poles and embroidered fabrics above her head.

She'd never really considered herself fit to be Queen of Narabia, but now she'd proved it beyond a doubt. Not just to her parents, but to a man who—as much as she wanted never to see or think of him again—she had a bad feeling had left an imprint on her body and soul she might never be able to forget.

As dawn fired across the horizon, Kamal galloped towards the rocky ridge which marked the edge of the Narabian desert, his destination the Azeala Oasis. He had managed to bribe the location out of one of the palace staff as the place where Kaliah Khan might be hiding.

The little coward.

The low-grade fury which had been riding him for over twenty-four hours—ever since Zane Khan had informed him oh, so casually that his honour meant nothing—now felt like a boulder jammed in his throat that he couldn't dislodge.

He'd attended all the foolish events laid on for the guests yesterday, hoping to corner Kaliah Khan in person and inform her that, whatever her father had said, he would not let her off the hook so easily.

So what if the news of their night together never left the Golden Palace? He would know what he had done—what *they* had done. What it felt like to feel her swollen flesh stretching to receive him...to take a man's body for the first time.

Shame, fury and a weird sense of possessiveness engulfed him again. The deed was done. And it couldn't be undone. Plus, he needed to find a wife this weekend. And, however unsuitable she was, she would have to be the one. Because he'd been so preoccupied with her, he hadn't had the headspace, or frankly the inclination, to pursue anyone else.

He hit the top of the ridge and tugged on Asad's reins to survey the land below him.

The morning light illuminated the encampment and the oasis below. The sunrise turned the water to a flaming orange to match the flicker of torches which had burned down during the night.

Was she really here alone, as the stable hand had suggested? Surely it was not safe for her to stay in such a place without an armed guard? He circled round, approaching the encampment from behind, and spotted in the corral the thoroughbred horse she had been riding in the race, munching on its feed-bag.

The mare's ears pricked up as Asad approached.

Kamal patted his stallion's neck to stop him alerting Kaliah to their presence before he was ready.

Dismounting in silence, he draped the reins over the corral railing, then unhooked the bridle so Asad could get a well-earned drink. But he didn't remove the saddle. They could not stay here for their discussion. He'd noticed a weather alert this morning for the whole region, signalling the possibility of sandstorms this afternoon.

The storms were rare, but could be dangerous, especially in such an exposed position. And, anyway, he did not want their conversation interrupted by the need to flee back to the palace. He wanted her on his own turf—where he could get the answers he sought out of her without any interference. The choking fury closed around his throat again.

She had used him and then discarded him—he understood that now—because he was not of royal blood.

He yanked off his keffiyeh and dunked his head in the water trough. The cool water washed away the sweat but did little to cool the anger and frustration that had been building ever since he had woken yesterday morning, the need for her still pounding through his system.

A need which hadn't really abated in the last twenty-four hours, even though she had rejected him.

Perhaps he ought to wait for her to wake up but, as he strode towards the main tent, he discarded the idea. They'd gone past politeness a long time ago. And he would be damned if he'd treat her like some rare, exotic bird when he'd been inside her, when her fingernails had dug into the scars on his back as she'd clung to him and the heady sobs of her climax, the sweet scent of her arousal, had driven him into a frenzy.

This has nothing to do with your honour, or the Law of Marriage of the Sheikhs, or even your need to find a convenient bride. Stop kidding yourself. This is much more basic and elemental than that.

The thought echoed in his head as his groin throbbed and the choking fury was joined by the feeling he hated and thought he had conquered long ago—of shame, of vulnerability, of yearning, the longing for something he knew he could never have, could never deserve.

He cut it off. *Again.*

He had fought long and hard to leave that child behind and become a man of standing, of huge wealth, importance and position. And he was not about to let some reckless virgin make him feel like that rejected boy again, however desirable she was, however royal her heritage.

The irony that she had made him feel this way once before, when she'd been five and he fourteen, didn't escape him as he ripped open the tent flap.

'Kaliah, it is Prince Kamal,' he announced as he stepped into the cool, shadowy interior. 'If you think you can run from me and our responsibilities, you are wrong. You have five minutes to clothe yourself.'

It took several seconds for his eyes to adjust to the light. But, several minutes later, she had yet to come out of the bedroom—or even reply to his perfectly reasonable demand.

To hell with this.

He strode across the lavishly furnished space. 'Time's up!' he shouted, and marched through the curtains guarding the bed chamber.

As his gaze slanted over her empty unmade bed, and a lung full of her spicy, sultry, spellbinding scent fired through his system, his temper charged back.

He marched out of the tent, the last threads of his control fraying.

When he finally located her, it would be nothing

short of a miracle if he managed to prevent himself from flinging her across his knee and spanking her.

Liah sighed as the spring water gushed from the rocks and doused her in glorious cold. It was already warm, and would be scorching later, but she had a solar-powered generator here to keep the living quarters cool.

Her skin tingled and pulsed, alive and still far too sensitive from her night of debauchery. She would have to return to the palace tomorrow—her father's steward had contacted her on the satellite phone twenty minutes ago to tell her of the threat of sandstorms. Their data were suggesting she should be okay, but her father was insisting she return home or he would send out the guard to bring her back.

After all the trouble she'd caused in the last few days, she knew she'd have to comply. At least Malik had also told her Prince Kamal and his men had departed for Zokar that morning, so she didn't have to hide out any longer.

She tilted her face into the flow and let the invigorating stream sluice down her body.

You're not hiding from him. You're simply giving him time to make a dignified departure.

She turned to tiptoe back across the rocks, her drenched T-shirt and panties making her aware of places still tender from his forceful caresses.

But, as she stepped away from the splashing water, a deep, husky sound, like someone clearing their throat, reverberated in her chest. Her head snapped up so fast, she almost got whiplash.

Him?

Heat and panic fired through her system, swiftly followed by shock. And a strange out-of-body sensation which made her sure she had to be imaging the tall, dark shape of the man who had occupied her thoughts for two solid days standing by the water's edge. His muscular arms were folded across his broad chest and his long legs were akimbo, encased in dusty jeans and riding boots, as if he were braced for action. The short black robe he wore to stave off the heat caught on the breeze and swirled around him, making him look like an avenging angel… Or, rather, an avenging devil.

She stared, utterly transfixed, as the heat continued to ripple through her over-sensitised body… Perhaps she'd got more sun than she'd thought on the ride here yesterday. Her worst nightmare could not possibly be here, standing on the shore of *her* secret oasis, his dark gaze roaming over her features then sinking down to examine her breasts with insolent entitlement.

Her nipples chose that precise moment to swell and elongate, poking against the wet T-shirt like two Exocet missiles. And making her brutally aware of the fact she was not wearing a bra. She folded her arms over her breasts.

Don't freak out. He's a mirage—he has to be. This is all in your head, and your guilty conscience.

But then the devastating illusion spoke. The brutal command in his voice was far too familiar as his searing gaze shot her body temperature into the danger zone.

'Get out of the water, Your Highness,' he said, the

honorific dripping with contempt. 'We have a long ride ahead of us to get to the safety of the Zokari gorge before the sandstorms hit.'

She pressed her forearms into the yearning flesh of her cleavage to stop it throbbing, and tried to give him her *No way, José* glare, which she reserved for her younger brothers when they were being particularly annoying.

Unfortunately, her glare lacked the usual searing effect, the shiver of sensation, the aching swelling in her breasts and the tender spot between her thighs all throbbing in time to her erratic pulse.

Am I losing it? I must be.

'W-what are you doing here?' she managed, still hoping he wasn't really here at all and this was all some kind of lurid, erotic nightmare.

'Saving you from a sandstorm and ensuring you become my wife—not necessarily in that order,' he barked.

Okay, so either she *had* lost the plot, or he had.

'You have ten minutes to get dressed and pack what you need while I prepare the horses for our journey,' he continued, as if he were the lord of all he surveyed and she his subordinate.

Her rebellious spirit finally kicked in. *Think again, buster.*

'I'm not going anywhere with you,' she declared, still shivering, still aching, the dread starting to engulf her.

'This is not a negotiation,' he said, his tone tight with strained patience. 'If you will not keep yourself and your horse safe, I will do it for you. You now have nine minutes.' So saying, he turned and marched back through the palm trees, leaving her shivering, shaking and swearing profusely at his departing back.

Fine, she'd get dressed—because being virtually naked while she confronted him was not a good plan—and then she would tell him where he could stick his rescue and his ludicrous notions of marriage. *Again*.

'Read my lips—I am not going with you. The data suggests the sandstorm will not hit until tomorrow at the earliest, by which time I intend to be safely back at the palace.' The flush of colour on Kaliah Khan's face and her obstinate stance, not to mention the loose robe she had donned to stay cool in the sun, was not doing a damn thing to calm Kamal's temper. Nor was the image of her exactly eight-point-five minutes ago with her pert nipples visible through the clinging fabric of her soaked T-shirt.

He had found her at the pond all but naked, her slender curves only accentuated by the drenched cotton. And, when she'd turned to him, he had become fixated on the plump flesh beneath. Her large, puckered areolas had been clearly visible and had only become more pronounced as he had stared, imagining them hardening beneath his tongue.

The sight had made his erection painful, which would make the six-hour ride they had ahead of them to get to safety even more fun. The sexual frustration had only added to his fury. How could she take such risks, to bathe as good as naked in the middle of the desert? There were few bandits in the region now, but anyone could have come across her.

'Get on your horse or I will put you on mine,' he snarled, clenching his jaw so hard he was amazed he did not crack a tooth.

Modern weather data could be useful, but it often lied. He could already smell the tinge of sulphur on the air, could feel the first tendrils of wind and see the dark red rim around the sun, now fully risen above the horizon. He would always trust his own instincts first and his gut was telling him they needed to leave now. But he would be damned if he would explain any of that to her. She did not respect him, or his instincts, so he refused to pander to her tantrum.

The woman continued to glare at him, stubborn, infuriating and proud.

'No,' she hissed.

The single forceful word snapped the last ragged thread on his patience and self-control.

She shrieked as he reached for her and began to kick, gouge and shout angry words he had never before heard come from the mouth of a woman. But he ignored her struggles, her protests, and ducked to avoid the worst of her slaps and punches—he was a trained fighter, forged in the fires of battle, and no mere slip of a woman would be able to best him, however strong her anger.

Clasping her around the waist, he threw her over one shoulder and marched across the corral as she struggled. He dumped her onto the powerful stallion's back.

Asad's head jerked sharply. Kaliah's scream was followed by more swear words as she grasped the horse's mane to prevent herself from falling. It kept her hands conveniently busy as he unhooked the reins from the post and mounted behind her. His aching groin bumped against her backside as he banded a controlling hand around her waist to draw her securely into his lap.

The horse reared, unfamiliar with the double weight, but Kamal controlled him easily with his knees. He felt the jolt going through her slender body, her teeth clicking as Asad's front hooves landed back on the parched earth.

'You…you bastard!' She gasped, but she sounded less angry now and more stunned.

He doubted anyone had ever sought to tame her before him, and he did not kid himself he had won. But her efforts were feeble now as she tried to prise his arm loose, her whole body shaking with the effort it was costing her to fight his far superior strength.

The scratches on his arm and his cheek stung as he spurred the stallion, who had been bred for endurance, into a gallop, whistling to ensure her mare, who he had already untied and saddled, followed them.

Kaliah shouted more obscenities at him, continuing to struggle and scratch but, as they galloped further from her camp towards the mountainous border region, he could feel the fight draining out of her. The struggle to stay on the powerful horse eventually became too much, even for her prodigious temper.

He slowed after an hour, knowing the punishing pace was not good for the horses in the rising heat, any more than it was good for his unruly passenger.

She sat stiffly against him, her body rigid with tension even though he could feel how exhausted she was, her ragged breaths making her breasts heave against his controlling arm.

Her silence seemed even more deafening than her earlier shrieks of protest.

But he didn't care. She could sulk all she wanted. He would have her where he wanted her now. The Zokari gorge would provide a natural shelter from the storms, and he had a lavish, well-stocked encampment there which he used to get away when the pressures of his new position became too much. So they would have peace and privacy for the conversation they needed to have.

He would make her understand he refused to be treated with such contempt. But, more than that, he would show her he was not a man who could be dismissed and discarded.

She still wanted him. He knew that much. And, once she had admitted as much, he would show her how a marriage between them could benefit them both.

'My father will kill you when he finds out what you've done,' she said finally, on a husky breath of outrage. 'You have just made a formidable enemy. I hope you realise that.'

'Your father will thank me,' he said, not disturbed by her threat. Khan would be furious, but he had only himself to blame for raising such a wayward, unruly child. And if this meant a stand-off between them, so be it. He would not back down again. 'For teaching you what it means to be a queen,' he continued. 'It is time you learned to observe the responsibilities that your position demands, instead of behaving like a wild girl who can do anything she wishes without consequence.'

She remained silent and rigid. An hour later, she began to sink into exhaustion, her body slumping against his despite her best efforts to hold herself apart from him.

A spurt of admiration went through him, despite the trouble she had caused him and the torn skin still smarting on his cheeks and forearm.

For all her wild ways, Kaliah Khan was a fighter.

She had fallen into a fitful sleep, her back resting against his chest, by the time they reached the entrance to the gorge, the rock faces shielding them from the worst of the heat.

He directed Asad up the rocky slopes, over the parched riverbed and into the trees. When they finally reached his encampment, she was too shattered even to lift her head. He carried her into one of the bedroom tents and laid her down on the pile of cushions. She rolled away from him—no doubt deliberately.

He waited until her disdainful shoulder lifted and fell in a steady rhythm again, then strode from the tent to prepare food and tend to the horses. And to clean the scratches on his face.

When she awoke, they would eat, then he would insist she trim her nails. And after that he would leave her alone. Even if it killed him.

Eventually, she would have to come to him—for they would remain here as long as it took for her to see reason.

But as he took the saddles off Asad, then Ashreen, fed and watered them both then cleaned their hooves and gave them a rub down, fatigue began to drag at him too. The adrenaline rush of the journey and the tussle beforehand had subsided to be replaced by a strange sense of uneasiness.

He had never physically manhandled a woman in his life. And, although he had only done what was necessary to bring her to safety and protect her from herself, the unsettling feeling lodged in his gut. Finding meat and a selection of vegetables in the camp's cold storage, he began preparing a stew for their supper—as the memory of her voice, sharp with resentment and anger but also tinged with hopelessness, pushed at a place he thought he had sealed off long ago.

The place where he had locked the deep sense of injustice which had nearly destroyed him as a boy, when he had been beaten, abused and told he had no right to make choices of his own by that bastard Hamid.

It is not the same.

He sprinkled flour on the meat and set it in the pan over the campfire.

Kaliah Khan has led a privileged, charmed life. She has never had to fight, never had to endure the contempt and disrespect of others. She has always been loved, cherished and indulged. It will do her no harm to be shown she can't have everything her own way all the time.

But as he watched the stew bubble, and threw in a few herbs and spices, he found himself dwelling on her refusal to look at him, even to speak to him. And the feel of her, so wary, so guarded, so tense and fragile, in his arms.

He was not good at interpreting other people's emotions because he had never had the luxury of examining his own. And he saw no purpose in regretting actions already taken.

But as the sun sank beneath the cliffs above them and the air chilled, his simple plan to rescue Kaliah, to bring her here and then set about showing her a marriage between them was destined and necessary, didn't seem quite so simple any more.

CHAPTER SIX

LIAH JERKED AWAKE, groggy, sore and angry. It took her several moments though to remember why she was not in her own tent at the Aleaza Oasis…and then the memories flooded back. Kamal's shocking appearance at the pool, the battle to stop him from putting her onto his horse. She'd screamed, kicked, punched and struggled against his hold with every ounce of strength she'd possessed. But he'd subdued her with disturbing ease, and an even more disturbing indifference to her rage.

He'd thrown her over his shoulder, dumped her on his horse—which had nearly thrown her in the process—and swung up behind her, his hard chest pressed against her back like a brick wall, banded one unyielding arm across her midriff and then galloped away with her without a thought to her feelings, her needs, her wishes or desires.

He had treated her like a disobedient child. Maybe he'd been careful not to hurt her and had in no way fought back against her tirade. But so what? She was a grown woman who had the right to make her own decisions. And he'd ignored that.

He's kidnapped me.

She shuddered. She had no idea where she even was. He'd mentioned something about a gorge. Were they in Zokar? What if he tried to force her into an arranged marriage? How the heck would she stop him?

Panic bumped against her breastbone as she raced through every possible scenario, each one scarier and more horrifying than the last. She breathed through it, her head starting to ache with the struggle to remain calm, focussed and decisive.

Zokar might not be as developed as her father's kingdom, but it was not unsophisticated. Just like that of Narabia, the economy had thrived in the last twenty years after the decision to mine its vast mineral wealth and it had begun to open itself to the world.

She thought of Kamal, dressed in a tuxedo at the Race of Kings reception. And later, in his bed-chamber, as he had stroked her to orgasm with a care and attention she had not expected. He was not an uncivilised man, however badly he had behaved this morning.

She had to believe that.

Her head continued to ache, along with every other part of her anatomy after their never-ending ride.

Stop panicking and start thinking, Liah. Because you're the only one who can get yourself out of this mess.

But as she glared at the ceiling of the unfamiliar tent, and the circular hole in the top used to allow cooling air into the space, it was hard to keep the fury at bay when it replaced the panic. Shooting stars flared across the inky blue above, a flash of brightness which instantly flickered and died. Unlike her temper, which was liable to blaze for a long time to come.

Stolen!

There was no other term for what he had done to her. Because she had not gone with him willingly—and she had certainly made that crystal clear in every way she could.

Perhaps he'd convinced himself he was rescuing her from a possible sandstorm. Kidnapping her for her own good, or some such nonsense. But they both knew that was just an excuse. And a pathetic one at that.

The storm wasn't due to hit until tomorrow—and, even if it had hit today, she would have been fine. She'd seen the storms before, maybe not in an encampment, but the desert tribes survived them so why shouldn't she?

Rolling over, she forced herself out of the bed, found the facilities at the back of the chamber and washed the trail dust off her face.

He'd left her clothed, at least, although her riding robe was now filthy and sweaty. In the outer chamber she found the bag she'd packed intending to head back to the palace. She dressed quickly in a pair of loose trousers and a T-shirt, then caught the scent of something rich, spicy and delicious.

Her stomach growled like that of a starving lion.

The realisation she hadn't eaten since the night before did not help control her fury because that was Kamal's fault too. But she hesitated before charging out of the tent to demand to be fed and then returned to the Golden Palace, ASAP.

For once, you need to be strategic.

Having a temper tantrum now would just give Kamal another excuse to treat her like an unruly kid. She took several deep breaths which, while they didn't do much to control her fury, did manage to stop her from marching out all guns blazing and giving the man who had kidnapped her yet more reasons to be a self-righteous jerk.

She lifted the tent flap slowly, to survey her surroundings.

She spotted Kamal instantly, crouched by the camp fire about ten feet away. His handsome features looked even harsher and more unreadable in the orange glow of the firelight.

Handsome? When did you start thinking he was handsome? He's not handsome—he's a flipping kidnapper.

But even so she felt the familiar flicker of reaction as she studied him.

'Know your enemy' was something she'd read in books, but it felt remarkably appropriate now if she were to have any chance of getting out of this mess without ending up unintentionally married, or triggering an international incident between Narabia and its nearest neighbour.

As much as her first instinct was to flee the first chance she got later tonight, saddle up Ashreen while Kamal slept, find her own way back to Narabia and her family and forget this had ever happened, she could already see that course of action was fraught with danger.

She didn't know where she was. She had no means

of navigation. And, despite having a first from Cambridge in the politics and history of the Nazar Desert kingdoms—which encompassed Narabia, Zafar, Zokar and the surrounding land—she had absolutely no experience of life in the desert, apart from the occasional overnight stay in the luxury accommodation supplied by her father.

She could die, lost out in the desert alone. And even she wasn't reckless and impulsive enough to put her life in danger—no matter how mad she was right now—which meant she would have to find a way to reason with the man who had kidnapped her. A man who seemed about as reasonable as a force-ten hurricane.

He didn't look her way, although she knew he had sensed her watching him from the way his stubbly jaw clenched.

She took the opportunity to study him, unobserved. The first thing she noticed was the way he was squatting on his haunches. It looked uncomfortable. But she'd seen her uncle Raif, the ruler of the Kholadi tribe, sit the same way whenever he was with his tribesmen. He'd once told her it was the most comfortable way to sit if you wanted to stay cool.

Did Kamal's stance provide some clues to his mysterious past? Strangely, despite her fury with him and the way he had treated her, her curiosity hadn't abated in the slightest. But maybe that was a good thing, because it might help her to figure out a way to persuade him what he'd done was abhorrent. And, given his arrogance, she suspected she was going to have an uphill battle persuading him anything he did was not okay.

She wasn't sure she'd be able to talk to him tonight without losing her temper, though. She was still too angry with him.

Her stomach chose that moment to growl so loudly, she suspected it could probably be heard back at the Golden Palace.

His gaze shifted to hers, the intensity in his eyes ripping through her hard-won composure to the girl beneath who had always refused to bow to any man— even her father most of the time.

And she respected and loved her dad.

Prince Kamal, not so much.

He stood, lifting off his haunches to his full height. He wore an open shirt and a pair of loose-fitting riding trousers, but his feet and head were bare and his hair was wet.

'You must eat,' he said, in that commanding voice which made it clear this wasn't a suggestion, it was an order.

Part of her—a very large part of her—wanted to tell him to get lost. But she was starving, the stew smelled delicious and there seemed no point in starting another argument until she was at least well-nourished enough to withstand the shudder of awareness playing havoc with her heart rate.

What is that even about?

So she strolled to the fireside, sat on one of the rocks and sent him a level look that she hoped conveyed how furious she was with him—as well as the fact that, just because she needed to eat before her stomach turned inside out, she had not forgiven him in any way, shape or form.

To her astonishment, he seemed to get the message, because he served up a generous helping of the stew and handed it to her without another word.

Their fingers touched as she took the bowl. She jerked her hand back, shocked by the visceral sensation that flared through her system.

Her gaze rose to his to find him watching her with the same dark intensity she remembered from their first night. He didn't smile, didn't really react at all. Though somehow she knew, in that patient, unreadable expression, he had felt the brutal awareness too but he was just better at controlling his reaction to it.

Great.

The vulnerability she had tried so hard to hide seeped into every corner of her being alongside the unwanted and uncontrollable reaction to the simple touch.

She tried not to bolt down the stew but, apart from the fact she was starving and it was delicious, she was suddenly desperate to get back to the relative safety of her tent. To regroup and start figuring out a strategy— not just to get him to take her back to her family, but how to handle the traitorous arousal.

After everything he'd done, how could she still desire him? Was this Stockholm Syndrome? A result of the stress of the last two days, ever since she'd sneaked out of his bed in the middle of the night?

But, as she sat beside him in the firelight, her body continued to yearn for his touch. And it occurred to her getting out of this mess was going to be much harder than she had assumed. Because he still seemed to have a strange command over her body, which she had no control over whatsoever, despite the appalling way he'd behaved.

And that could be bad. In fact, it could be very, very bad. Because it was that same visceral reaction that had helped get her into this enormous mess in the first place. And she suspected he knew how to use it against her. So getting to know him better was fraught with all sorts of risks she hadn't even considered.

What if her curiosity about him—that odd feeling of connection, of sympathy for the battles she suspected he had fought for so much of his life—brought an intimacy she also couldn't control?

Oh, boy, I'm so screwed—and not in a good way.

Leaving the last few bites of the stew, because her appetite had suddenly deserted her, Liah dumped the bowl and spoon in a water vat he had placed beside the fire then got up and marched to her tent without another word.

He didn't stop her.

Perhaps he was expecting her to thank him, maybe even to offer to wash up. Well, he could forget both. She was here against her will, and she did not plan to have another conversation with him until he had apologised and offered to take her home.

Refusing to engage with him, and this enforced camp-out, was her least worst option. Or rather the only strategy she'd come up with so far.

As she tied up the tent flap to make it crystal-clear she did not want a visit from him tonight—or any night—her fingers shook. Because she had a bad feeling Prince Kamal might well be the most stubborn, intractable and taciturn person she had ever met. And that meant their stand-off could last a very long time.

Way to go, Liah. This is turning into your most epic screw-up ever.

CHAPTER SEVEN

YOU'RE GONNA NEED a new strategy.

Waking up on the morning of day three of her enforced camp-out, Liah finally admitted the silent treatment was not working. She'd spent approximately forty-eight hours giving Kamal the cold shoulder and he didn't even seem to have noticed, let alone tried to communicate.

She'd assumed he'd eventually come to her, if only to demand she do her fair share around the camp. She'd had a whole speech ready and waiting for that moment, which she had edited and re-edited in her head about five thousand times—explaining in words of one syllable exactly why what he had done was wrong and what the consequences of his actions would be if he didn't return her to Narabia pronto.

But he'd outsmarted her, because they'd barely exchanged three words in the last three days, and she was about to burst with frustration.

Instead of demanding she help out, or even bringing up the question of their first night and his demand they marry, he had been stoic and uncommunicative. All the while he'd taken care of the horses, cooked their meals, cleaned up and then disappeared for most of the day on his stallion.

She'd taken Ashreen out for an exploratory ride the day before while he'd been away—hoping against hope that maybe she wasn't as far from Narabia as she'd thought. But, after an hour-long ride to the end of the gorge, she'd scanned the desert plane beyond that they must have traversed during the long ride to get here with a pair of binoculars she had found in the camp's supply tent. The terrain was rugged and inhospitable, and she hadn't been able to locate a single familiar landmark or rock formation.

Forced to return to the camp, she had expected Kamal at least to say something about her decision to venture out without his permission. She'd almost hoped he would be mad at her so she could finally force him to confront the seething atmosphere simmering between them—and deliver her damn speech. But he had simply stared at her. For a split second she had thought she saw relief in his eyes, but she was sure she must have imagined it when, saying nothing, he had handed her a plate of the fried meat and rice he had been eating, and then returned his attention to his own meal.

She glared at the open hole in her tent roof, the morning sun sprinkling the bedchamber's lavish furnishings with a golden glow, as her anger built at his apparent indifference to her whereabouts yesterday.

Who was giving whom the silent treatment here? Because it seemed that, after two long days and nights, he was winning the damned sulk-off she had started, which just infuriated her even more.

How on earth was she supposed to deal with a man who was so flipping contrary? What exactly did he even want from her? Why had he brought her here, if not to try and coerce her into marriage?

Throwing off the fine linen sheets, she marched to the wash basin to cool down. As she sluiced the water over her face and chest, she ignored the low-grade hum that had been pulsing over her skin ever since Kamal had discovered her bathing at Aleaza four days before. The low-grade hum that flared every time she spotted him in the camp, or woke up hot, sweaty and unbearably aroused every night troubled by erotic dreams…

Curtailing her wash so as not to encourage the hum, she strode to her pack and pulled out the last of her clean clothing. *Terrific.* She didn't even have clean panties for tomorrow, when she had no doubt at all they would probably still be here, busy avoiding each other like a couple of grumpy teenagers.

Her father would surely be looking for her by now. She needed to inform him where she was. And for that she would have to speak to Kamal.

First things first—you need clean panties before you figure out a whole new strategy to get Prince Hard Head to see the error of his ways.

She knew there was a water source nearby—she was pretty sure Kamal used it to bathe. She'd avoided it herself. She did not want to give him another chance to find her in a compromising position.

The hot spot between her thighs throbbed on cue at the memory of the last time he'd caught her bathing.

After dressing in her jeans and T-shirt, she strode

out of the tent to find the camp empty and no sign of Asad or Kamal anywhere. He must have gone on his daily ride.

As she grabbed the pile of dirty clothing, her temper simmered at the thought of all the freedom he enjoyed that she did not. She could wash the clothes through, while coming up with a new strategy to finally deliver her speech without compromising her autonomy or giving him any hints about the stupid hum!

After checking on Ashreen, who she discovered had already been fed, watered and exercised by Kamal that morning, she headed through the ferns and palms that surrounded the camp, following the thin trickle of water in the nearby riverbed until she caught the sound of running water—and the scent of jasmine and desert sorrel.

As the trail took her deeper into the gorge, its red walls towering over her, the rocks turned to sand and the stream widened.

The splashing sound became louder as she finally passed through the last of the trees and found a sandy cove that surrounded a wide, deep pool of iridescent blue.

The splashing noise came from an impressive thirty-foot waterfall that tumbled into a pool at the far end of the gorge. She took a moment to take in the stunning beauty of the natural pond, the urge to strip off and dive into the cool blue all but unbearable.

This pool was much larger and more dramatic than the pond at Aleaza, lapping against the inland beach on one side and the base of the red rock-cliffs on the other.

But, just as she debated stripping off for a quick dip, she heard a nicker. Kamal's horse walked through the trees at the other end of the beach. The magnificent stallion wasn't wearing a saddle or bridle as it dipped its head and drank thirstily at the water's edge. The sheen of sweat on its rump and flanks suggested the horse had been ridden hard—and apparently bareback—not long before.

Is Kamal here too?

She should go back to the camp. But somehow she couldn't seem to turn and retreat, her thundering heartbeat sinking deep into her abdomen.

Then Kamal's dark head surged out of the water ten feet away. She eased back into the shelter of the trees, spellbound as she watched him swim in fast, efficient strokes towards the waterfall. The glimpse of tight buns had her heart jamming into her throat and sinking down to throb painfully between her thighs.

He's naked.

Her gaze remained glued to him as he ploughed through the water towards a rocky outcrop beneath the falls.

Go back now, before he spots you and the hum becomes completely unbearable.

But she couldn't move, couldn't even detach her gaze, as he planted strong hands onto the lichen-covered rocks and levered his strong body out of the water.

Her avid gaze trailed up long hair-dusted legs roped with muscle and over the smooth, paler rounded orbs of his exceptional gluts. But then her eyes widened and her heart slammed into her chest wall as her gaze reached his back.

The breath she hadn't realised she'd had trapped in her lungs gushed out on a shocked gasp, then the pulsing ache charged up from her core and wrapped around her ribs in a vice. The copper-brown skin, so muscular and strong, was marred by a criss-cross of scars, so many scars.

'Oh, no,' she whispered as the backs of her eyelids burned.

Even from this distance she could see the raised marks clearly. The ragged strips covered the whole of his back, stretching from the broad ridge of his shoulder blades all the way down to the base of his spine. She stared, her breath clogging in her lungs, recalling the strange ridges she'd felt when she'd clung to him as he thrust into her. Ridges she'd been curious about but had never seen because of the shirt he'd Insisted on wearing.

He reached up to slick back his hair and step into the stream of water pounding down from the fissure in the rock wall. The torn flesh on his back flexed and stretched.

These were old scars which had healed long ago. But, even so, she couldn't swallow down the well of sympathy building under her breastbone at the evidence of the violence and abuse this hard, indomitable man had once endured.

Knowing exactly how strong he was now—thanks to her own first-hand experience—she knew no one could have done this to him as an adult.

Was that why he hadn't removed his shirt during their night together?

The wrenching in her chest became worse.

Kamal was a proud man. She'd convinced herself he was too proud—willing to ignore her wishes, and even his own, to satisfy some arcane tradition, some stupid sense of honour. She swallowed to ease the thickness in her throat and the thundering pain in her ribs. It occurred to her his pride, his determination to do the right thing after he'd taken her virginity, might have nothing to do with tradition, honour or even his new position as a desert prince and everything to do with the boy who had once been so brutally beaten. Was that the real reason his pride meant so much to him?

She retreated into the undergrowth—suddenly feeling like the worse kind of voyeur—and retraced her steps along the rocky path back to the camp, the bundle of dirty clothing forgotten in her arms. Her heart continued to pulse at her throat but, instead of fading, the thickness in her throat became raw and jagged as one of her earliest memories flickered at the edges of her consciousness. An encounter she remembered from long ago, when she'd been a little girl, and she had made eye contact with a serving boy while on a diplomatic visit to Zokar with her father and her uncle Raif.

She had never forgotten that boy—although he hadn't seemed like a boy to her then, because he'd been so much older than her. But, as she recalled him now, she realised he could only have been a teenager, tall, wiry and way too thin, and no match for the brute who had appeared from nowhere and attacked him when he had dropped a few plates.

She could still hear the hideous thud of the belt slicing through flesh, the man's angry shouts and the boy's strange grunts as he had lifted his arms to stave off the attack. Could still hear her cries of distress as she had begged her father to intervene—and stop the awful punishment. And she could still see her father leaping up to grab the man's arm and prevent him from hitting the boy again.

Recalling that terrifying incident, and how her father had reprimanded that horrid man and spoken quietly with the boy to ensure he was okay, her love and respect for her father swelled.

But the swell of respect and affection for her father was nothing compared to the surge of distress and pity she still felt for that boy...

And her shock at the look in his eyes when his gaze had connected with hers that day. She could still picture his face as clearly now as if that incident had been yesterday, not fifteen years ago—the sallow skin, the high cheekbones hollowed out by malnutrition and the deep amber of his eyes sparking with anger, resentment and fierce pride. But what had shocked her most of all was the lack of tears, even though she'd been able to see blood seeping through the worn fabric of his shirt.

She blinked furiously, aware of the sting behind her eyes again.

From the first moment she had met Kamal something about him had seemed strangely familiar. And now she knew what it was. His eyes were the same deep amber as that boy's eyes, and they'd had the exact same expression in them, four days ago in her father's study, when he had demanded marriage and had been told no.

As night fell over the gorge, Kamal led Asad along the trail back to the encampment, his skin bristling from his second cold swim of the day, after yet another hard ride through the canyon to try and alleviate at least some of the sexual frustration that had been threatening to blow his careful plans to have Kaliah come to him for three endless days now... And even more endless nights.

How much longer is she going to ignore me and the incessant heat between us?

The heat he'd been able to see in the flush of her skin as she'd sat across the fire from him and eaten the food he had made for her wearing a sour, angry expression on her face.

He had spent the last two days venturing further and further away from the camp on Asad so he would not have to spend time close to her. And had forced himself to trust she would not try to leave again after he had tracked her to the edge of the canyon yesterday. He had been prepared to follow her into the desert, if she tried to cross the deadly terrain. But, as he had watched her through the spyglass while she'd assessed the desert beyond the gorge, he had seen her shoulders slump and the defeated look on her face.

Pride had risen in his chest alongside the ever-present frustration. Kaliah Khan might be impulsive and reckless—and far too captivating—with a temper that could put an unbroken stallion to shame but she was not a fool.

Even so, when he had left the camp today, determined not to return until nightfall—for his own stress levels as much as hers—the fear she would do something reckless had not helped to control the unsettled feeling that was now a permanent fixture in his gut.

Last night he had stopped himself from touching her, from goading her, from demanding to know what the hell she had been thinking, believing she could survive in the desert alone. Not just because he wanted her to feel less of a prisoner but also because he could not trust himself not to go too far. The desire to glide his fingers over the swell of her breasts, pluck those responsive nipples, nibble across her collarbone and make her beg was something he was becoming increasingly concerned was liable to drive him wild.

He huffed out a breath, the heat pumping back into his groin.

Damn. Stop thinking about the scent and texture of her skin and the soft sobs which drove you mad on that one night with her in your arms or you will need yet another cold swim.

Asad snorted as they entered the camp. Kamal tied him alongside Ashreen in the corral. He patted the mare's back, surprised to see new feed had been added to her bag and the stall had recently been mucked out.

A small smile creased his lips.

Finally. Kaliah was relenting. Surely this had to be a sign she had decided to stop sulking? Perhaps tonight he would be able to coax her back into his bed and prove to her that a marriage between them would have some benefits.

Although the need to persuade her to marry him felt a lot less urgent than it had three days ago. His concerns now almost exclusively centred on the need to get her back into his arms and for her to forgive him for the high-handed way he had got her here.

He frowned as he rubbed down the stallion, poured fresh grain into its feed bag and replenished the water in the corral's trough. Not that he needed to be forgiven. He had done what was necessary for her safety as well as his future. Was it his fault she still had some growing up to do?

He stopped abruptly though as he walked out of the corral, surprise swiftly followed by the pulse of longing.

Kaliah sat beside a newly built fire, the simple outfit of jeans, boots and a T-shirt doing nothing to disguise her long legs and small but perfectly formed breasts. Her tawny skin—glided by the firelight and the gathering twilight—glowed with health and vitality.

The heat surged in his groin and he let out a harsh grunt. So much for the long day spent away from her, and the cold swims. Her head swung round and their gazes locked. He smelt it then, the aroma of cooked meat and spices.

Had she made supper for them both?

Something he did not really understand pressed against his ribs. He had many chefs at the palace in Zokar who could conjure up the most delicious dishes. And then there were the servants at his home in the foothills of the tribal lands. He had employed them primarily to cook for him. Because he had gone to bed hungry so many nights as a boy, he had promised himself one day he would always be able to afford to have the best food, the richest food, whenever he wanted it.

But no one had ever cooked for him before now, without being paid to do so. And he certainly had not expected such domesticity from Kaliah, when she probably still hated his guts.

He took in another lungful of the spicy aroma. In truth, he was also astonished she knew how to make a meal in the desert—perhaps she wasn't as pampered as he had assumed.

She stood as he approached the fire and tucked her hands into the back pockets of her jeans in a nervous gesture which made the worn cotton stretch over her breasts.

He studied her face, expecting to see anger. Her expression was flushed and wary, but there was no fury in the crystal blue.

'I figured it was my turn to make us supper,' she offered, surprising him even more.

He nodded. 'It smells good.' He forced the words out past the dryness in his throat, aware that this was the first conversation they had had without rancour since their first night.

Her tongue flicked out to lick across her bottom lip, the gesture one of nerves. But still he felt the shock of arousal. The tension ramped right back up again, but this time it was as exhilarating as it was frustrating.

'Take a seat,' she said, gesturing towards a place

on the other side of the campfire. 'And I'll serve you a bowl, so you can tell me if it tastes good too.'

He didn't want to sit so far away from her. But the truce—after so much animosity—felt too fragile to test, so he did as she asked.

It occurred to him, as he hunkered down and watched her intently while she ladled a generous helping into one of the earthenware bowls, he had never shied away from rancour or animosity before. He was used to fighting for what he wanted and was more than prepared to meet fire with fire, confident in his ability to do whatever was necessary to win.

But he'd used brute force to get her here four days ago. And for once the process had left him with doubts he had never experienced before. Doubts not so much about the result—he would never have left her alone with a sandstorm forecast—but rather the method. He was still convinced it had been necessary, but could he have used more finesse, more subtlety? Did he even know how?

He had never been a particularly erudite man. And he had no experience of flattering or cajoling women, especially women who required more than what he could offer them in bed. But the fact he had taken her choices away from her had left him feeling oddly unsure every time she had glared at him as if she wished to peel his skin from his bones.

Her virginity had disturbed him greatly once he had discovered it—for the simple reason he had convinced himself it would mean they must marry. But, over the last three days, something else about her virgin state had begun to disturb him a great deal more. Why had she chosen him as her first lover? Why had she trusted him with something so precious, when they were virtual strangers?

And had he done enough to deserve that trust? The thought that he must have done only concerned him even more. Because her trust felt like something precious he had earned unwittingly, and then discarded far too easily the next morning in her father's office with his demand for marriage... And which he had ultimately broken beyond repair with his decision to take her from her homeland.

He took the bowl from her, absorbing the ripple of reaction as their fingers brushed.

She scooted back around the campfire to sit on her allocated rock, rubbing her palms against her jeans. He dipped his head and concentrated on digging his spoon into the fragrant stew to hide the smile curving his lips.

Why was he complicating this? Desire was the reason she had chosen him—the chemistry they shared had been obvious from the start. The only difference was she had no experience of such a connection. No ability to deny it.

But you've never felt a connection this kinetic and all-consuming either. And you have a great deal more experience than she does.

The smile died as he shovelled a spoonful of stew into his mouth and the rich, earthy flavours burst on his tongue.

Stop over-thinking this. She is precious. But this relationship is about sex, first and foremost, and necessity.

He spent the next five minutes eating, letting the heady flavours fill his belly and ignoring the tender space that had opened inside his chest at the thought she had made this meal especially for them. For him.

Kaliah Khan was no fool, and as he finished off the stew, scraping the last of the gravy from the bowl, it occurred to him what this truce was really about.

It was a bribe—pure and simple. But her wish to barter was something he could use. Because communication was always better than silence when it came to negotiations.

With his belly pleasantly full, and the flicker of firelight making his skin pulse and glow, he dumped the empty bowl into the water vat he kept by the fire and stretched out his legs.

Their gazes connected again and he let the desire charge through his system unchecked as his gaze roamed over her.

'That tasted as good as it smelled,' he murmured, his voice husky with hunger of a different kind.

'I'm glad,' she said.

He searched for calculation in her eyes but saw none. Perhaps she was warming to him. Good—it would save time if she had finally accepted a marriage between them would not be such a terrible thing. If there was a way for them to both get what they needed, he intended to find it. Tonight.

'So tell me, Your Highness,' he murmured, feeling confident about his approach for the first time in days. 'Is there anything you would like from me in return?'

Liah saw the hot light in Kamal's eyes and the promise of pleasure only he had ever fulfilled. Need ricocheted through her over-sensitised body. She was playing with fire now. She got that, because a relaxed and self-satisfied Kamal Zokan was even more dangerous than a furious or dictatorial one.

Who knew?

But, even so, she couldn't stop the question she had been waiting to ask him ever since that morning from bursting out of her mouth.

'Why didn't you tell me we had met before when we were children?'

He stiffened and straightened against the rock, no longer smug. But the guarded look in his eyes, and the wary tension which made the muscle in his jaw jump, told her all she needed to know. She had been right. The man who would soon be King of Zokar and that abused serving boy were one and the same person.

His gaze became hooded. 'I do not know what you refer to,' he said evasively, but the defensive tone only confirmed her suspicions.

Her father had told her Kamal had an unusual background for a prince, but she'd had no idea he had managed to gain the throne after such a tough start.

Apparently he seemed determined to hide the fact, though. But why?

She huffed out a breath, the nuclear blush from that morning's realisation heating her skin all over again as he studied her intently. She was going to have to reveal why she had recognised him all of a sudden.

Terrific.

She swallowed past the dryness in her throat then blurted out the truth.

'I went to the pool this morning to wash out some of my clothes. But you were already there…bathing.'

His gaze narrowed, the feral light in his eyes making the heat flare at her core. But with it came the flicker of shame.

'You…you had your back to me,' she added.

The muscle in his jaw twitched as he clenched his teeth. 'You spied on me?'

She broke eye contact. 'Yes, I guess I did. And I'm sorry.' She forced her gaze back to his despite the guilt prickling over her skin. 'Something about you always seemed familiar, ever since we first met at the track.'

She gulped down the blockage in her throat as he simply stared at her, his expression deliberately blank. 'But I couldn't put my finger on it. Probably because I'd met you so long ago. But when I saw the scars on your back, it all came back to me. That afternoon during our state visit to Zokar. The serving boy who was so brutally punished by his employer for such a minor infraction. The violence shocked me at the time, probably because I'd led a rather sheltered life.' She was babbling now, but she couldn't seem to stop, her heart in her throat as he stared at her, the blank expression making the ache in her stomach so much worse.

What must it have been like to be treated with such casual cruelty? How had he survived it? Had there been no one to protect him? What had happened to his parents?

'I had nightmares for years afterwards about that incident,' she continued, suddenly desperate to get a reaction out of him, or at least an acknowledgment.

'But one thing I never forgot was that boy's bravery. His refusal to be bowed. He seemed so fierce and proud to me.' She took in a deep breath and let it out slowly. 'Why didn't you tell me that boy was you?'

Did he despise her, resent her, because she had led such a pampered life compared to him? In some ways she would understand that. Was that why he had ignored her for the last four days? She felt embarrassed now that she hadn't offered to help out around the camp and had left him to do all the work. At the time it hadn't been a status thing—not at all—it had been a temper thing. But she could see how it might have seemed very different to him.

Her parents had always told her brothers and her that their heritage and wealth did not make them better than anyone else. That the role of royalty was one of dignity, service and duty. But she'd screwed up with Kamal—behaving like the spoilt brat he'd accused her of being without intending to—right from the first moment she'd met him... And suddenly she wanted to take all that back, to start over, to prove to him she'd never thought she was better than him. And had certainly never believed she was too good to marry him. If anything, the opposite was true. She had always been a screw-up and now this proved it.

'I would never have thought less of you,' she continued, probably sinking even further into the ginormous hole she'd already dug for herself, but unable to stop digging. 'For being that boy. I hope you believe me.'

Kamal stared at the earnest expression on Kaliah's face, her compassion worn like a badge of honour. It triggered a strange warmth in his chest he had never felt before. And frankly didn't want to feel.

But as the miasma of conflicting emotions boiled in his gut—shock, anger, pain, humiliation—he had no idea how to respond to her.

A part of him wanted to continue to deny he was the boy she remembered. Because it made him feel brutally exposed in a way he hadn't felt since he'd been that boy. No one knew the whole truth of his origins, not even the tribal elders. *Especially* not Aziz. If they did, his early life—as an orphan, a mere serving boy—might be used as another reason to deny him the throne.

What sickened him the most was the thought of her seeing the scars he had kept hidden for so long. But what shocked him was that, instead of thinking less of him, she appeared to think more of him. Was this some kind of weird fetish she had, to befriend the downtrodden? Or simply a clever trick to gain his confidence and co-operation?

But, even as he tried to galvanise his temper, he couldn't make himself believe there was anything calculating or condescending about her declaration. Her expression was far too forthright, and more open than he had ever seen it, and her words rang with an integrity that seemed genuine.

He stood, agitated and disturbed. He walked round the fire, then clasped her wrist to tug her off her rock until she stood toe to toe with him. The dark compassion in her eyes didn't falter as she searched his face—still looking for answers, still trying to see that valiant boy who was long gone.

He cupped her cheek and dragged his thumb across her lips, unable to resist for a moment longer the temptation to touch her again that had been driving him for days.

She jolted, her gaze flaring with awareness now, as well as the deep compassion that was doing strange things to his stomach muscles.

Desire flared, potent and provocative, providing a handy escape from the raw emotion in her eyes.

'I did not tell you because that boy died a long time ago,' he said, his voice gruff with an emotion he didn't want to feel.

Her eyes widened and it occurred to him he had just revealed something to her he had never revealed to another living soul. Hamid had died not long after he had joined the army and, after he had resigned his commission and made the investments which had made him a wealthy man, he had erased his past. He'd literally had all the records of his apprenticeship and his early life at the orphanage in Zultan destroyed.

'Did he?' she whispered, the approval in her gaze making his insides clench with a longing he hadn't felt in many years—to matter to someone other than himself. She covered his hand with hers, her gaze rich with a fierce emotion he did not understand.

He didn't want to be that boy. That boy might have appeared fierce and proud, but in reality he had been weak and pathetic. He had allowed himself to be beaten and abused, had made the mistake of wanting someone to care for him.

'I'm not sure he did, Kamal,' she said.

The betraying glow in his chest spread through his system but he braced against it.

He hated that she still saw that boy. And that she might understand him in ways that boy would once have yearned to be understood, but which the man knew were fundamental weaknesses.

He breathed in her scent—that intoxicating aroma of fresh water, salty sweat and the sweet musk of feminine arousal.

He threaded his fingers into her hair, clasping the back of her skull to lift her face to his.

'Do not mistake me for that boy, or I will have to prove I am very much a man,' he murmured against her lips.

Arousal flared, turning the crystal-blue of her irises to black. She shivered, her reaction like that of a wild horse ready to be tamed.

Anticipation surged, turning the threatening warmth to scorching heat.

Then her lips parted in an instinctive sign of her surrender. It was all the invitation he needed to slant his lips across hers and plunder.

CHAPTER EIGHT

LIAH OPENED HER mouth as Kamal's tongue thrust within—commanding, devastating but also desperate. She let the giddy ache build, pressed her body to the hard unforgiving contours of his and absorbed the thrill of connection, of yearning. And ignored the small voice in her head telling her to be careful.

She needed this, needed him…because he needed her too. She could feel it in the rasp of his breathing as his tongue delved and possessed. She grasped his shirt in handfuls to drag him closer as his callused palms roamed down her back then cupped her backside, making her brutally aware of the ridge in his pants.

He lifted her into his arms, dragging his mouth from hers. 'Wrap your legs around my waist.'

She did as he demanded without an argument, surrendering to the madness. He marched them through the camp site towards his own tent. Firelight flickered in his dark eyes as she continued to kiss him—pressing her lips to the scar on his cheek, his stubborn chin, the fierce frown on his forehead.

Perhaps she should have been worried about what

this all meant for them both—especially after what had happened the last time she'd made love to this man. But this didn't feel like a surrender, it felt like a meeting of equals.

Whipping away the tent flap, he headed across the luxurious space, drenched in moonlight. Starlight sparkled through the hole in the tent roof, magical and romantic. Her breath hitched at the strange beauty of the setting. But the enchantment faded, becoming more urgent, more elemental, as he placed her on her feet beside his bed.

He ripped open his shirt, flung it away then got to work on his trousers.

'Undress, Kaliah.'

The harsh command made her shudder, but again she followed his orders, tugging off her T-shirt, slipping off her boots and jeans and scrambling out of her underwear—until they stood naked, only inches apart.

His chest looked even more magnificent than she remembered it, but as she curved her fingers over one broad shoulder she touched the ridges on his back. He shuddered, his gaze intensifying—the flash of vulnerability so vivid for a moment, her chest tightened, even as need shuddered to her core.

Her heart expanded, her breathing laboured, as she drew her fingers down his chest, brushing over the flat nipples, trailing through the thin line of hair which bisected his abs, until she got to the thicket at his groin.

He let her explore, standing stoically as he allowed her to touch, tempt and tantalise. She discovered other scars—a small one across his left pec, another mark slanting over his ribs, one more that grazed his obliques. How could she have been so preoccupied in her own pleasure not to have noticed them before?

Her heart pulsed harder. So much pain, so much suffering. She absorbed the evidence of the hard life he had led, all the damage he had endured.

His erection stood out, long and thick, the swollen head shiny with his need.

She glided her fingernail over the tip and he groaned as the strident flesh leapt towards her touch.

Excited, exhilarated, she swallowed past the dryness in her throat, suddenly desperate for the taste of him, desperate to show him she could appreciate everything he was—the man as much as the boy.

She sunk to her knees in an act of reverence and supplication. But as she looked up and saw him staring down at her—the flare of passion in his gaze as surprised as it was intent—her own power surged.

'Kaliah,' he moaned. 'You undo me.'

Taking him in her hand, she wrapped her fingers around the thick girth then licked him from root to tip.

He groaned, the sound so low, guttural and tortured it felt as if it had been dragged from the depths of his soul. The salty taste of him thrilled her, and the power became intoxicating as she kissed and caressed the erection with her tongue, her teeth, her lips—finding how to make him moan, how to make him ache, the way he had once done to her.

At last, she opened her lips as wide as she could and sucked him into her mouth. He grasped her head, his whole body trembling with need now, his hips moving as he stroked his length into her mouth.

She lapped up every sweet sensation, every shuddering grunt. But suddenly his fingers dug into her hair to drag her back.

'No more, or I will lose myself...' He groaned.

Taking her arms, he yanked her back to her feet, then plundered her mouth again.

Could he taste himself on her? The thought was so erotic, the swell of power became all but unbearable.

They fell onto the bed together, a tangle of limbs, a battle to hold, to taste, to touch every inch of flesh.

He kissed her breasts, stroked her sex, as she continued to caress him wherever she could reach.

He reared back, then flipped her onto her belly to drag up her hips and position her on all fours. She jolted as the huge head of his erection nudged at her entrance from behind.

'You are so wet for me, Kaliah,' he said, the pride like a benediction. He dragged the erection through her swollen folds, rubbing, teasing. She quivered, bracing for the devastating thrust, but it didn't come. She bucked as his erection nudged her swollen clitoris— the touch almost enough to send her over. But then he withdrew.

'Tell me you want all of me,' he demanded. And somehow she knew he spoke of that battered boy as well as the indomitable man.

'Yes... Yes, I do...' She groaned, so desperate now she couldn't breathe.

At last he pressed within, the all-consuming thrust

forcing her forward, but he held her firmly as he anchored himself to the hilt.

She could feel him everywhere. Her body clamped down on the thick intrusion. She felt impaled, possessed, conquered. Her chest heaved, the power still there but somehow rawer, more carnal, more basic.

Then he began to move, rolling his hips, drawing out of her, pressing back, forcing her to take every vital inch. His chest pressed against her back, his hands cupping her breasts to hold her steady for the ruthless, relentless thrusts.

She sobbed and begged…for him to go faster, harder, to take her all the way. But he kept the same steady pace, each slow, devastating thrust taking her further to that edge, but building her higher, until she was sure she couldn't take any more.

'Please… I can't bear it!' she cried, the pleasure so intense now it robbed her of breath, of power, until all that remained was the throbbing bundle of fraying nerves, the endless yearning.

'Yes, you can, you must,' he commanded, his voice as wild as her own.

She reached down to touch herself, to end the torment, but he grasped her wrist, preventing her. Then he touched her there, where she needed him the most, sweeping over the yearning point with brutal accuracy.

The coil inside her cinched tight and then released in a rush. The pleasure soared and shattered—so sharp, so hot—burning up from her core and sweeping through her body like a comet.

She massaged the thick erection as the searing orgasm pulsed through every nerve-ending, every pulse point, exploding into a conflagration so bright, so bold, she felt the touch of it in every recess of her heart, her soul.

He pumped into her, his shout matching her cries as his seed flooded her womb. And she let herself fall.

Kamal groaned and rolled off the woman beneath him. The chemistry was still incendiary between them—maybe too incendiary.

Nothing could have prepared him for the sight of her, on her knees before him, taking him into her mouth. For the feel of her lips as they'd closed around him.

His heart jolted at the memory. Her gaze as she had stared up at him had been so strong, so determined—every inch a queen—and yet also so full of that fierce compassion, it had nearly unmanned him.

She sat up beside him with her back to him, then shifted away, as if she were about to leave his bed.

'Don't go…' he said, grasping her arm, the words harsher—and more needy—than he had intended.

She glanced over her shoulder, then sent him a guarded, almost shy smile that made his heart thunder against his ribs. 'Okay,' she murmured, settling back into his arms.

He gathered her close, deciding not to question the urge to hold her—an urge he had only ever had with her. After all, he intended to make this woman his wife—and soon. He had shown her precious little tenderness so far… Perhaps it was time for him to dig deep and find that part of himself he had discarded to survive.

He felt strangely content as he cradled her back against his chest and pressed his face into the fragrant curls that haloed around her head.

But, before long, the liquid weight pooled again in his groin, making him harden against her bottom.

'Don't get any ideas, buster,' she said, her voice sleepy. 'You've exhausted me.'

He let out a gruff chuckle—enjoying the way she always stood her ground.

'Ignore it,' he said. 'I have no control over my reaction to you,' he added, surprised—and a little concerned— to release it was the truth, and another first with her.

He gathered her wild curls in his fist to place a kiss on her nape. She shuddered in response, and a fierce sense of possessiveness flowed through his veins.

'I did not use protection,' he said. 'Will this be a problem?' he asked, even though it would not be a problem for him. If she were to become pregnant, it would only help his cause. The thought of her slender body heavy with his child sent an erotic charge through him that felt completely disconnected from his desire to make her his queen.

'Are you healthy?' she asked with a directness that surprised him all over again.

He caressed her neck with his thumb, tracing the graceful line down to her shoulder, unable to stop touching her. Perhaps he should be offended, but somehow he found her bluntness refreshing and beguiling instead. Was that the afterglow too?

'Yes, I am healthy. I have never taken a woman without protection before now,' he admitted, realising this was yet another first. He traced his fingers down her side, then settled his hand over her flat stomach, imagining a child—*his* child—growing there.

Fierce pride joined the possessiveness.

Children had always been an abstraction before now. He had accepted he would have to provide heirs as part of his responsibilities to the Zokari throne, but the thought of Kaliah Khan having his son—or daughter—made it seem so much more real. And something he found impossibly arousing.

She would be his then. Always.

'My concern is only about a possible pregnancy,' he added, wrestling the conversation back to where he wished it to be. He'd always intended to use protection. The explosive passion in the moment had ensured no thinking had been done at all. But now the chance of a pregnancy seemed fortuitous. And a golden opportunity for him to press his case.

She sighed, then threaded her fingers through his to draw his hand away from her belly. 'There's no need to worry. I'm on the pill.'

Disappointment flooded him, and he frowned.

'Why is this so?' he asked, something hot and uncomfortable piercing his happy glow. 'When I am your first lover?'

She stiffened in his arms and glanced over her shoulder. The indignation in her eyes contradicted the blush on her cheeks somewhat.

'I'm fairly sure that's none of your business, Kamal,' she said.

Of course, it is my business. You are to be my wife.

He bit down on the thought. It was too soon to press her on this. Then she added blithely, 'But, just for the record, you weren't my first lover.'

Okay, this is too much.

'How is this so when we both know you were a virgin?' he demanded. Was she playing games with him again, trying to pretend she had not been untouched?

'Again, not your business,' she said, pulling out of his arms and scooting off the bed. 'I think I should return to my own tent. This was obviously a mistake.'

She scooped her T-shirt off the floor, tugging it over her head.

He jumped up to snag her wrist before she could run from him again.

Her eyes widened as her gaze shifted to the strident erection that he could not disguise. The vivid blush flared across her collarbone as her eyes met his.

'I'm not sleeping with you again, Kamal,' she said. 'So you can just get that idea right out of your head.'

'I told you to ignore that,' he shot back. 'I would never force myself on a woman,' he added, his own temper rising. 'But I wish you to tell me—if I am not your first lover, what did you do with the others?'

The jealousy blindsided him, making the words spill out, and reminding him painfully of that boy who had always needed validation, approval, when it had never been forthcoming.

'Did you get on your knees before them too? Did you make them ache, the way you made me ache?'

Liah twisted her wrist out of Kamal's grasp and glared back at him. But her fury was tempered by her panic. Kamal Zokan was formidable—and even more annoyingly hot—when he was being a possessive, macho jerk. His chest heaved with indignation—and he was apparently completely unembarrassed by his nakedness and that strident erection.

What the hell?

The truth was, she'd never got past kissing any of the boyfriends she'd had in school and college. She'd gone on the pill six months ago when it had looked as though she and Colin were getting serious, until she'd overheard him talking to one of his friends about her.

'She's a frigid bitch, but she's gorgeous, and she's going to be a queen one day. So I'm more than prepared to suffer for the cause.'

Maybe he had been joking, but the joke had been on her. She'd thought he liked her, for herself. That he found her exciting and interesting. But he'd been manipulating her all along, and laughing at her, because of who she was—and what he could get out of her. It had sickened her and upset her. How could she have trusted such an idiot? They'd been going out for four weeks and she'd never guessed that he was like all the other men and boys she had dated, only interested in her because she had status and wealth that they craved.

What had hurt most of all was that Colin had never

even excited her that much, but she'd been willing to go all the way with him to discover if there could be more.

With Kamal, though, it had always been different. There hadn't really been much thought to any of it. She'd been swept away on a tidal wave of yearning, and so had he. Or at least that's what she'd assumed.

But now, once again, she was unsure of herself. She'd thrown herself at him tonight, believing they had made a connection when she'd recognised the boy behind the man. Someone vulnerable who had struggled with their position in the world, something she could relate to. But now she wasn't so sure, because he looked every inch the desert prince again. A man who took what he wanted and wasn't interested in intimacy or emotions.

One thing she did have to thank Colin for, though, was the fact she was using contraception, because until Kamal had mentioned, oh, so casually, that he hadn't suited up, she hadn't even considered the possibility of an unplanned pregnancy. She had been way too steeped in afterglow and had become stupidly sentimental about the feel of his strong arms cradling her—even the press of that enthusiastic erection against her bottom—to worry about anything other than when she was going to get her next endorphin fix.

But she'd come crashing back to earth, with a vengeance. Because he was looking at her as if he owned her, and as if he had a right to expect an in-depth history of her sex life. Something she had absolutely no intention of giving him, because it would make her look and feel pathetic. They wouldn't be equals any more. But had that been an illusion too—the power she'd thought she'd wielded?

What had she been thinking, giving in to him again? His outrageous questions though, deserved an equally outrageous answer.

'If you're asking me whether I've had oral sex before,' she said, slapping a hand on her hip and trying to look a lot more experienced than she actually was, 'I'll let you figure that out for yourself.'

She'd loved kissing him, touching him, caressing him. She was proud of the fact she had made him ache. But he'd made her feel cheap and used now. He'd taken all the power away from her. And she hated him for it.

She swung round, planning to march out of the tent, glad she'd got in the final word. But he leaped forward, grasped her arms from behind and wrapped his strong body around hers. Suddenly she was trapped, sensations she couldn't control streaking through her again.

'Let me go,' she murmured, trying to struggle free, the tears she refused to shed making her throat hurt.

'I am sorry, Kaliah.' The gruff apology shocked her—almost as much as the feel of his arms softening and then releasing her. 'I was jealous. It is a new experience for me.'

She gulped in several raw breaths, the emotion still pressing against her chest but, when she turned to see the haunted look in his eyes, she was stunned.

He cradled her cheek in his palm, the calluses rasping against her skin. She should pull back. They were having an argument, and he still had that possessive gleam in his eyes. But she couldn't seem to draw away from his touch, or deny the thundering of her heart-beat. No man had ever looked at her like that before, with such intensity.

'I know you have not done such a thing for another man,' he said.

She blinked, trying to push her temper back to the fore. 'How do you know that? Wasn't I any good at it?' she demanded, feeling insecure again, and hating it.

Colin had called her frigid. And, as much as she'd hated him for it, she had always been a little scared it might be true.

But Kamal simply laughed, the chuckle releasing the tension that crackled around them. 'You are far *too* good at it. Which is why I am honoured you chose me to experiment with.'

She could deny it, of course. Pretend she had experience she didn't. But her throat closed on the lie as she braced against the warm glow in her chest, the stupid sense of validation. She didn't need this man's approval. So why did it mean so much?

His thumb glided down to capture her chin and lift her face to his. 'Am I wrong?' he asked, his tone coaxing now.

She looked away from him, the gentle question making her throat tight again. She blinked furiously, unsure about why she was becoming so emotional.

'Why does it matter?' she replied, feeling weary and defeated. 'It's not as if I'm *your* first, now, is it?' she added, the indignation brewing again.

'This is true,' he said, making her feel even more deflated. But then he slipped his finger into her hair and hooked the unruly curls behind her ear, forcing her to look at him again. 'But you are very different from the other women I have been with.'

'How?' she asked, hating the neediness in her voice, but wanting to know.

'I cannot really explain it,' he said. 'We have exceptional chemistry, but also...' He paused, as if he were searching for the right words. 'You are my first too in many ways.'

He frowned, and she suspected he had said more than he had intended to. The warmth spread in her chest, but she pushed it away, not quite able to believe he meant it. Was he trying to flatter and cajole her? He had always seemed like a very blunt man, but she knew he still wanted to marry her, so there was that.

'Is it because I will one day be Queen of Narabia?' she asked, deciding to put him on the spot.

Was he like all the others? Attracted first and foremost to her status, wanting her for *what* she would be one day, not who she was now? She felt the dart of pain in her stomach, knowing that somehow it would be so much worse if Kamal was like the rest.

His brows shot up his forehead, the puzzled expression on his face making relief course through her, and then he laughed. 'You are already a queen, Kaliah. The Queen of Trouble.'

A chuckle burst out of her mouth at the outrageous statement. But something about the playful smile on his lips—something she already knew was rare, because he was an extremely serious man most of the time—made her heart bounce.

'Fair point,' she said.

He laughed again, the rough, rusty sound impossibly beguiling, then reached out and captured her hand in his. 'Come back to bed. I promise I will not ask you any more questions. Let us lie together. I wish to have you in my arms when I wake tomorrow,' he said, the flirtatious light in his eyes another surprise, but no less compelling. 'And you robbed me of this on our first night.'

She knew she shouldn't encourage any more intimacy between them, but she couldn't find the will to object when he led her back towards the bed.

Now they were actually talking again, she would have to press him about contacting her father first thing tomorrow. She should explain to him the danger he was putting himself in if her father discovered he had kidnapped her.

But as she climbed into the bed with him, and allowed him to tuck her against his chest and hold her, contentment settled over her. She could feel his heart thumping against her back in heavy thuds, feel the still firm erection nestled against her bottom—and the feeling of connection she had never shared with another man overwhelmed her.

It was an illusion, of course, a result of the fact he had been her first. But it felt good to know she wasn't the only one who had been altered by their encounter. She doubted she could ever be friends with this man, but as she drifted into a deep, exhausted sleep—her body tingling insistently in all the places he had touched and caressed—it felt as if sex wasn't the only thing that connected them.

Kamal saw her in a way no other man ever had. Not just as a sexual being, but also as an equal, different from the other women he had known, in the same way he was so different from the men she had known.

And that felt important…and precious. Somehow.

CHAPTER NINE

WHEN LIAH JERKED awake the next morning, she found the bed empty beside her and the sound of distant rumbling in the air.

Was a thunderstorm coming? And where was Kamal?

She dressed hastily in the clothes scattered around his bed chamber and rushed out of the tent, her heart pumping double time when she spotted Kamal standing with his back to her, staring down the gorge.

The rush of euphoria turned to panic as she realised the rumbling was the sound of horses' hooves echoing off the canyon's walls.

She reached Kamal's side just as her father appeared, galloping towards them on his stallion Zufar, leading a column of at least fifty men.

She grasped Kamal's arm. 'Let me speak to him, Kamal,' she said urgently over the noise of the approaching army. 'This could get awkward.'

Kamal's brows furrowed. 'I am not afraid of your father, Kaliah,' he said, placing his hand over hers. The touch of his palm sent sensation skittering.

She tugged her hand out from under his—the possessive gleam in his eyes not helping with her anxiety attack.

Terrific—just what I need. My endorphins playing tricks on me when I need to come up with a plan— fast—to save Kamal from the consequences of his actions.

He'd brought her here against her will, but she knew now he wasn't a bad man, just an impulsive, impetuous one who tended to act first and think later.

She took a step away from him, just as her father leapt off the powerful stallion and strode towards them.

'Liah, thank God! You're safe,' he said, then dragged her into his arms.

She clasped him around the waist and let herself be held, aware of the shudders wracking his tall, lean body.

When he drew back at last, and held her at arm's length, she was shocked by the worn, weary expression on his face.

Her father was her rock—a man who never faltered, never lost his cool…at least not completely. But his hands were shaking as he clasped her upper arms, the look in his eyes one of utter relief.

'You're not hurt?' he asked, his voice breaking.

Guilt seared her insides. She'd known he would be concerned she hadn't returned sooner from the oasis, but she hadn't expected him to be quite this frantic.

'No, I'm fine. I'm sorry I didn't come home sooner…' She swallowed, trying to explain why she was in Zokar—and had been for four long days. Although she was a little surprised her father hadn't already confronted Kamal. 'There's no mobile phone service here, so we weren't able to let you know where we were,' she said lamely.

He cradled her cheek, then to her surprise let out a wry laugh. 'It's okay, Liah, I'm not mad, just incredibly grateful you survived.'

Survived? It was her turn to frown. *Survived what, exactly?*

Before she could even formulate the question, her surprise turned to astonishment when her father turned to Kamal and clasped his arm, before shaking his hand vigorously. 'Thank you for saving my daughter. My family and Narabia are for ever in your debt.'

Kamal nodded, apparently completely unfazed by the conversation. 'There is no debt to be paid. It was my honour to protect Kaliah.'

I'm sorry—what now?

She'd expected her father to be furious, to demand to know what the heck Kamal had done, bringing her to the gorge—and keeping her here against her will. And, while she had been more than prepared to lie on his behalf, to protect him from any repercussions, now that Kamal and her were, well, friends of a sort, her father's decision to completely absolve him was a little aggravating, frankly.

'Excuse me, but what exactly did he rescue me from this time?' she asked, testily, interrupting the developing bromance.

Her father's eyebrows hitched up his forehead, then he frowned. 'The sandstorms, of course,' he said, looking at her now with something less than extreme relief.

'Four major storms converged on the region the afternoon after you headed to the oasis—we had to declare a national emergency. Your mother has been coordinating relief efforts in Narabia while I've been searching for you. Nearly half of Raif's tribal lands were hit. Two people died in Zafar from sand inhalation when it swept through there, and it buried the encampment at Aleaza. I thought you were under it, until we received word that Prince Kamal had made a detour *en route* back to Zokar to check on you.'

He thrust his fingers through his hair, his drawn face making the guilt sweep through Liah again—this time on steroids.

Good grief. Kamal really had rescued her this time by insisting they leave the oasis. And she'd had no idea. Sandstorms were very rarely deadly, but she would have been alone and completely unprepared in the middle of what sounded like the worst storms for a generation. No wonder her father had been so frantic. He had to be exhausted too.

'I'm so sorry,' she said, horrified at her own selfishness. Her father had been trying to find her, when he would have wanted to be in Narabia to coordinate relief efforts himself. Could she actually have screwed up any more comprehensively than this? *Doubtful.* 'Is everyone okay in Narabia?' she asked. They were her people, people she was one day supposed to rule, and yet she'd let them down again by going AWOL. And she'd had no idea.

Nausea joined the lump of shame forming in her throat. Her father had told her a week ago that not everything was about her. Perhaps it was past time she stopped thinking about herself—stopped panicking about how she would ever be good enough to be a queen and actually began behaving like one.

'The repair bill is going to be enormous, but no one was badly hurt, which is the only thing that matters,' he said.

'Dad, I'm so, so sorry.' She flung her arms around his waist again, buried her head against his sturdy chest and breathed in his familiar scent—leather and horses. The tears lodged in her throat like boulders.

He wrapped his arms around her, so solid, so strong, so dependable.

'Hey, Liah, it's okay,' he said as he kissed her hair, in a way she remembered him having done so many times before, ever since she'd been a little girl when he'd always praised her out of all proportion to her achievements. 'We've found you and you're okay, that's the main thing,' he finished as he gave her a final squeeze.

She pulled back, swallowing furiously to contain the emotion pushing against her chest.

Kamal stood stoically beside them, saying nothing. But she spotted the confusion in his gaze before he could mask it. And it made her feel so much worse.

She had always had her father's approval, her family's unconditional love and support, even when she'd done nothing to earn it. While Kamal had had no one to protect him from that awful man who had beaten him. Everything he had, he'd had to fight for, while she had never had to fight for anything.

She'd fought her destiny for so long, even resented

the fact she, and not her brothers, would one day be expected to rule Narabia. It was way past time she stepped up to the plate and began to earn at least some of her father's respect.

So when her father frowned, his gaze going back and forth between the two of them, she decided she would do anything necessary now not to make this situation worse.

'Just out of interest, Kamal, why *didn't* you return my daughter to the Golden Palace several days ago?' he asked, his gaze probing now as his euphoria at finding Kaliah began to fade.

As grateful as her father had been to Kamal moments ago, Zane Khan was no one's fool. She could see his sharp mind shifting into gear. He had to be recalling the acrimonious way she had spoken about Kamal five days ago—and her determination to have nothing to do with him, or his proposal of marriage.

Uh-oh.

While her father was her greatest cheerleader, he was also her biggest defender and protector. She knew a part of him still considered her his little girl—despite all the evidence to the contrary in the past week—and all his gratitude towards Kamal would dry up in a nanosecond if he thought the neighbouring prince had taken advantage of her or the situation.

Think, Liah, think. Time to finally put your fledgling diplomatic skills to the test.

She needed to come up with a way to defuse the growing tension—a white lie that would adequately explain why they had apparently made no attempt to

return to civilisation after surviving the storm. Something appropriate and suitably innocuous that didn't involve her telling her father the truth…that she'd spent
last night in Kamal's bed. But then heat flared across
her collarbone, making her brain stall completely, just
as Kamal spoke.

'I did not return her because Kaliah is going to become my wife,' he said, managing to torch all her good
intentions in one fell swoop. 'We slept together last
night and she may be carrying my heir,' he finished,
throwing petrol on the fire and turning an awkward
situation into a raging inferno.

Kamal heard Kaliah's horrified gasp beside him. Her
father's eyes narrowed as his blue eyes—so much like
his daughter's—became chips of ice.

Kamal lifted his chin, more than ready to stand his
ground. Khan was a powerful man, both in the Nazar
region and the wider world, and Kamal could see he
was not happy about this development.

But he'd be damned if he would bow to any man—
especially on his own land. He had stopped bowing and
scraping and being ready to settle for scraps as a boy
of sixteen, when he had finally escaped from Hamid
and enlisted in the Zokari army. Maybe he was not of
noble birth, but that did not make him a lesser man than
Zane Khan. And he was more than happy to prove it
to Khan and the small army he had brought with him.

'You did *what*?' the Sheikh snarled with barely
leashed fury—the fierce gratitude of moments ago
apparently obliterated by Kamal's statement of facts.

So be it.

The man's gratitude had made him uncomfortable anyway. After all, he considered it *his* duty to keep Kaliah safe now, not her father's.

'You heard me,' Kamal shot back.

'Kamal, stop it!' Kaliah cried, pushing between the two of them and bracing her hands against his chest. 'Please, just stop talking, you're making this so much worse.'

'I will not stop talking. I am telling the truth,' he said.

'Just for the record, did my daughter have a choice in any of this?' Khan shouted.

'Are you accusing me of rape?' Kamal demanded, as his own temper incinerated the last of his control and his fingers tightened into fists.

The Sheikh's men dismounted to circle them, ready to intervene if Khan requested it. Kamal's temper flared, the tension on a knife-edge.

He was outnumbered and outflanked. But the fury strangling him refused to subside.

For many years, all he had had was his honour. And Khan had just questioned it. *More* than questioned it.

'Dad, it's okay, I had a choice!' Kaliah's frantic cries finally pierced through the hot rage rushing in Kamal's ears. 'What happened last night was one hundred percent consensual. Kamal would never do something like that.'

Khan's gaze jerked to his daughter, although the fury still vibrated through his body. And Khan's men were still watching, ready to do as their sheikh demanded.

But all Kamal could see in that moment was Kaliah.

Her fierce defence of him sent shockwaves through his body. He had not expected it. He would never have believed it would matter so much to him but somehow it did.

'You don't need to defend him, Liah,' her father said, clasping her arms, searching his daughter's face again to see if she was hurt, the way he had when he had first arrived. 'If he took advantage of you, or kept you here against your will, that's on him—not you. And he will pay the consequences. And you're certainly not obliged to marry him, even if you are pregnant right now, I hope you know that.'

Kaliah's gaze shifted from her father's face to Kamal's. And what he saw in her gaze had the shockwaves turning into something harsher and even more disturbing—releasing a depth of emotion he had never felt before, touching that open wound in his stomach he thought he had cauterised so long ago. The wound that had always been there when he'd been a boy, every time Hamid had taken a belt to him, or he recalled the hazy memories of the man who had left him sitting on the steps of the orphanage as a young child. A man he had convinced himself in the years since must have been his father. The father who hadn't wanted him.

Kaliah looked so strong in that moment, but the wary knowledge in her gaze spoke volumes.

He braced, prepared for her to tell her father the truth—that he *had* brought her here against her will.

That he had kept her here without offering to return her so he could persuade her—by whatever means necessary—to marry him. They had slept together last night because their chemistry was off the charts, but how much of a choice had she really had when he was so much more experienced than she was?

Shame seeped through the layer of fury.

But when she spoke her words only shocked him more and sent furious longing through him which he could not control.

'Dad, Kamal's not lying,' she said, her voice trembling. 'He asked me again and I accepted. We're engaged to be married.'

CHAPTER TEN

'I DO NOT recall asking you to marry me again, nor do I recall you accepting my proposal, so why did you say this to your father?'

Kaliah swung round at Kamal's question.

Even in the shadowy interior of her tent she could see the frown on his face. He had his arms crossed over his chest and looked even more formidable than usual—which was saying something.

She sighed.

Great—just what I need. Another hot-tempered alpha male to placate.

She stopped stuffing the last of her belongings into the saddle bags she'd packed nearly a week ago, intending to escape from this man. A man she'd just spent half an hour trying to persuade her extremely sceptical father she was desperately in love with.

Thank goodness her father had finally agreed to let her travel to Zokar to make an official announcement about their 'engagement'. After feeding and watering their horses, her father and his men were now on their way back to the Golden Palace.

Diplomatic crisis averted.

Apart from the six-foot-four-inch crisis standing in front of her now, brooding magnificently.

Kamal had remained silent and watchful throughout her conversation with her father. But thankfully he had not contradicted her—nor had he intervened when she had insisted they needed to travel to Zokar to announce their engagement. Given his penchant for throwing petrol on any given situation, with his infuriating need to take charge of everything, she considered that a minor miracle in itself.

She had hoped Kamal's silence meant he had figured out she was lying through her teeth so they could avoid their little tryst in the desert leading to a major diplomatic rift between Narabia and Zokar, and that he was on board with her plan…

From the deep suspicion in his eyes, though, apparently not.

She dumped the saddle bag at his feet.

'Isn't it obvious?' she said, her own temper flaring. Seriously? What the heck had he been playing at, goading her father like that when he'd been outnumbered fifty to one—did the man have a death wish?

'Not to me,' he shot back.

'I was saving you, Kamal. My father was on the verge of withdrawing his support for your monarchy,' she snapped. 'You saved my hide at the oasis, so I was returning the favour.'

He tensed, the offended look in his eyes only making her more furious. So that was the deal? He was allowed to save her but she wasn't allowed to save him? *Figured.*

'So, it is a lie, then?' He sounded outraged. 'You do not intend to marry me?'

'Of course not—we'd probably end up killing each other within a week. Then both our sacrifices would be for nothing,' she said, letting every inch of her frustration show. Not just with Kamal, but also with her father, who frankly hadn't exactly covered himself in glory with his refusal to believe her for thirty frustrating minutes—while she had waxed lyrical about how much in love with Kamal she was, having known him for precisely six days.

She'd never been more humiliated in her life. But, as she crouched down to buckle the straps on her saddle bags with more force than was strictly necessary—while steadfastly ignoring Kamal, who was still glaring at her with that smouldering look of disapproval—she decided she had only herself to blame.

She'd got into this situation by making a ton of stupid decisions and it was her job to get herself—and Kamal, who appeared to be his own worst enemy—out of it. Perhaps the solution she'd come up with—faking an engagement between them until her father backed off—wasn't the best solution, but it was the best one she'd been able to conjure up on the spur of the moment before all hell broke loose.

'You expect us to travel to Zokar and announce an official engagement between us, but you have no intention of marrying me?' Kamal's words were laced outrage.

She let out a heavy sigh, her already knotted stomach twisting tighter, before she stood and faced him.

'I know it's not ideal, Kamal. But I had visions of the two of you coming to blows, which wouldn't exactly have been great for diplomatic relations, now, would it? I was scared, okay, and I was trying to defuse a situation which you managed to torch with that daft comment about me being pregnant. I told you I was on the pill—there is zero chance of me being pregnant and you know it.'

'Your father is not a fool,' he said, choosing to ignore her last cogent point. 'He would not have destroyed diplomatic relations with a neighbouring state over such a thing.'

'You don't know my dad,' she replied wearily. How could Kamal be so obtuse about this? But then she recalled that boy, fierce and proud but also so alone. Had he ever even had a father? Was that why he was so clueless about how family dynamics worked?

'My father's a strong ruler, and a good one—he's also a brilliant diplomat. But his family and his children mean everything to him. There's nothing he wouldn't do to protect us, to the point of being completely irrational if we are threatened in any way,' she continued. 'And I've never seen him quite so strung out. Plus, my mum wasn't here to help defuse the situation. So I did not want to take the risk, okay?'

The tell-tale muscle in Kamal's jaw twitched. 'I told you I was not scared of your father,' he said, completely missing the point. 'Did you think I needed you to tell lies on my behalf? Because I did not. It is not your place. I can protect myself. I always have and I always will. I have no need to rely on others to protect me.'

She simply stared at him, aware of the fierce pride bristling around him like a force field. Part of her wanted to shout at him. To get it through his thick skull she'd been trying to help him, not hurt him. But she could hear the confusion in his voice, right behind the fierce determination always to be self-sufficient, and recalled the hideous scars on his back.

Kamal's pride was clearly the only thing that had got him through the abuse he had suffered in childhood and had made him into the man he had become. Thick-headed, for sure, arrogant, autocratic, ruthless and everything in between. But also honourable and honest.

Plus, this man had saved her life with his pig-headedness. So there was that.

She heaved another sigh and tried to dredge up what was left of her flagging patience.

Hello again, newfound diplomacy skills.

'I'm sorry if I've put you in an awkward position,' she managed. 'But it really doesn't have to be that awkward. We certainly don't have to go through with the whole official engagement thing. I just wanted to get my dad to leave before anything bad happened to you. Or him,' she added hastily, the admission sounding somehow too intimate, too presumptuous.

His brows lowered still further. 'You were worried about me?' He sounded genuinely stunned. And her heart cracked at the thought of that boy who had only ever had himself.

'Precisely,' she said, willing to admit that much if it

would get Kamal to see she had never meant to insult him or trap him—perish the thought. 'But we really don't have to announce anything at all. We could just spend a couple of days together in Zokar, while my dad calms down in Narabia. Then I'll go home. Tell him we broke it off after all. That it was all just a silly infatuation on my part.' Which would make her look like even more of a romantic imbecile in her father's eyes.

But then maybe that was a good thing. Her father had always had far too much faith in her. Perhaps it was high time she began to downgrade his expectations and made him see she wasn't queen material.

Although, the thought of him losing his faith in her only depressed her more. Because, if this afternoon had taught her one thing, it was that she didn't have to be such a screw-up all the time. If she could start putting her duty and her responsibilities ahead of her impulsiveness, her recklessness and her own selfish choices, the way she had this afternoon, maybe there would be hope for her after all.

Kamal shook his head. 'This is not a solution.'

'Why not?' Liah asked, confused by the stubborn look on Kamal's face. She'd just offered him a way out of this mess, why wasn't he taking it?

'Our honour requires that we go through with the engagement now.'

Oh, for...

She pursed her lips to stop herself losing her patience again. Because it didn't help anything, especially not with Kamal, who only became more impossible when confronted. They were both hot heads, so one of them had to figure out how to back down gracefully… And, on this occasion, apparently it was going to have to be her.

'I don't think it does,' she said wearily. 'But, if you think it's necessary, I'm happy to go ahead with the announcement. After all, I was the one who suggested it. Then we can figure out a way to break off the engagement without arousing any suspicion at a later date.'

Perhaps this was another penance she deserved. A fair price to pay for the sense of entitlement she had never even realised she had relied upon her whole life. She hadn't considered Kamal's pride when he had first proposed marriage. She had far too easily dismissed the importance of his honour to him. Because her pride had never been questioned. Because her status—as the eldest child of the Narabian Sheikh—had never been in any doubt.

And, really, would it be so terrible to spend a few weeks posing as Kamal Zokan's fiancée, given that there were so many things about him she found fascinating?

Her skin flushed as his gaze gleamed with a purpose she recognised. Because he'd looked at her the same way last night before he'd kissed her so hungrily in the firelight.

He cupped her cheek, his voice becoming huskier as his thumb cruised over her bottom lip. 'Don't look so worried,' he murmured. 'There will be some very pleasurable benefits to our arrangement.'

She nodded. 'I know.'

Which was precisely the problem.

She was still drawn to this man, far too much. Even though their association so far—and that explosive chemistry—had caused them both nothing but trouble.

But somehow, as they prepared the horses and packed the rest of their belongings to travel to Zokar and announce their fake engagement, she convinced herself this arrangement would work.

Perhaps it was time she indulged the side of her nature which she had denied for so long, and which Kamal had triggered without even trying. Surely giving in to this chemistry would eventually wear it out? And, when they broke off their engagement in a couple of weeks' time, a month at the most, her father would have got over his anger with Kamal and she would have established a good working relationship—of a sort—with the ruler of Narabia's nearest neighbour.

It was all good.

Totally. All. Good.

After the primitive luxury of the camp, Liah couldn't help gawping as they galloped towards the prince's palace on the outskirts of the sprawling town of Zultan—Zokar's main city.

She didn't know what she'd expected, but certainly nothing this magnificent. Flanked on two sides by the red rocks of Zokar's mountain range, the palace had been built around a huge oasis. After being ushered inside the walls by an honour guard, they rode through an avenue of palm trees and exotic flowers planted beside an intricate series of fountains and waterways.

Liah's breath stalled again as the main palace buildings appeared, built into the rock wall of the canyon. Constructed in the Ottoman style, the stunning structure stood five storeys high, an intricate collection of domes, towers, minarets, arches, balconies and covered walkways—with decorative wooden ramparts that hailed the expertise of ancient craftsman and jewelled mosaic tiling that glittered in the sunshine.

She had no idea what she had expected, but certainly nothing this sophisticated or stunning. She realised she had never seen this place when she had accompanied her father on the state visit all those years ago. They had instead been accommodated in a tented encampment out on the plains. When had this palace been constructed? Because it looked at least as old as Narabia's Golden Palace, and equally as lavish.

The decision to fake an engagement with the new Crown Prince suddenly felt a great deal more complicated. Especially when a group of staff gathered to greet them as they rode through the palace's main domed arch and arrived in a smaller courtyard. A beautiful fountain stood as its focal point, the gold figurine in the centre shimmering as water spouted from its mouth and sparkled like rare gems in the sun.

A line of dignitaries appeared in full ceremonial garb, clearly having assembled to welcome their soon-to-be-crowned king.

Liah knew all about pomp and circumstance, having grown up a sheikh's daughter, but even so she stared wide-eyed as Kamal was greeted with great deference by men she suspected must be the ruling elders he had mentioned on the ride, when explaining to her how they would have to present the engagement.

'There will be expectations—just let me handle it,' he'd said with his usual authority.

After the scene at the camp with her father, she had been way too stressed to worry too much about what that might mean, until Kamal jumped down from his horse then marched towards her to help her off Ashreen.

She slipped down into his arms, shocked by the oddly proprietary gesture as he stared into her eyes, towering over her, and held her around the waist. Was he going to kiss her in front of all these people?

Her lips tingled, as her gaze dropped of its own accord to those firm, sensual lips that quirked now with a rueful smile.

'Do you wish me to stake my claim on you, Kaliah?' he murmured, his voice a husky purr full of amused arrogance.

'No, of course not,' she mumbled, jerking her head up and trying to tug herself out of his embrace. But he held her firmly, stopping her from retreating, the mocking light in his eyes suggesting he knew exactly how off-balance she was.

'We don't need to be quite *that* convincing,' she added breathlessly.

'Don't we?' he said, the amusement dropping from his expression.

Then, to her stunned surprise, he dropped his head to press his forehead to hers and breathed in, the gesture somehow even more intimate than a kiss. Suddenly everyone else faded away until it was just the two of them, cocooned in the rare chemistry which seemed to shimmer in the air around them like the glittering light on the palace's mosaic tiling.

Her heart pounded so hard, she was surprised it didn't beat right out of her chest as his callused palm settled on her cheek and then slid down to cup the back of her neck.

'We cannot sleep together at the palace unless we are wed,' he said, his voice so low only she could hear him. 'Tradition demands I show my future queen the ultimate respect.'

She nodded. 'Okay.'

That's probably a good thing. Surely sex—especially the kind of sex we have—would only complicate this situation more? I need to start weaning myself off this man now.

But even as she tried to persuade herself this new development was for the best, disappointment rippled through her system and weighed down the hollow ache in her stomach. Then his thumb caressed the hammering pulse point in her neck. She sighed before she could stop herself and he chuckled.

'Do not worry. I embark on a European trade tour tomorrow. You will come with me as my fiancée.'

What?

The information registered, delivered—as per usual—not as a question but a command. Even, so she struggled to get her mind to engage while the tantalising scent of him filled her senses.

'For…for how long?' she managed, knowing she

should object. A European trade tour had not been part of their agreement. And surely presenting herself as his fiancée on the world stage would only make things that much trickier when they called it off?

'Ten days,' he said, then skimmed his thumb across her lips, pressing down on her bottom lip and making the ache so much worse. 'I will insist we have adjoining suites. And no one will dare question our activities after the official business is conducted.'

'But…what then?' she murmured.

'Then we return to Zokar,' he said.

Ten days to indulge this insatiable passion before they went their separate ways?

Should she? Could she? Surely such an arrangement would be playing with fire? Hadn't she already been scorched enough?

She tried to open her mouth to clarify exactly what her official duties would entail. And to get a more robust commitment out of him regarding the parameters of their fake arrangement. For example, how long did he envision them lying about the engagement once they returned to Zokar?

But she couldn't seem to speak past the lump of anticipation and excitement forming in her throat…and making her panties damp with need at the thought of being so close to him for ten days. Having the chance not just to sleep with him every night, but to spend time with him in his role as the soon-to-be King of Zokar.

Perhaps she needed this. Perhaps they both did, to finally burn away whatever it was that had drawn them together so forcefully. Theirs had never been more than a physical connection. That was what she needed to remember. Why shouldn't they indulge it? After ten days, they would be more than ready to part, and her fascination with him would be over.

So she simply nodded. 'I guess I can do that,' she said, even though she knew full well he hadn't really asked her. He had told her.

His arrogance was something else they could work on in their ten days together, she thought ruefully as he dropped his caressing thumb to clasp her hand in his and lead her to the ruling elders, who were still hovering nearby, waiting patiently for their little *tête-á-tête* to end.

As they marched round the fountain together, Liah pushed her unruly hair back from her face, wishing she had at least had a chance to wash before making these introductions.

It doesn't matter, remember? You're not his real fiancée.

'Gentlemen, I present my future wife,' Kamal announced, the thick pride in his voice not sounding all that false. Who knew the man was such a persuasive actor? 'And the future Queen of Zokar, Crown Princess Kaliah Khan of Narabia.'

The men dropped into low bows, some of them even kneeling before her and genuflecting, a custom that had been done away with in Narabia during her father's rule.

But, as the ruling elders greeted her formally and congratulated her profusely on her new role, with a deference which made her feel like a total fraud, Liah could see the stunned shock on everyone's faces but Kamal's.

She knew just how they felt, because as Ashreen was led away by the palace grooms, and she was spirited away by a trio of new personal assistants and shown to a lavishly furnished suite of rooms in the women's quarters—where she was to spend the next twenty-four hours being 'prepared' for her first official engagement as Prince Kamal's bride-to-be—her fake engagement didn't feel at all fake any more.

CHAPTER ELEVEN

One week later

'LIAH, IT'S SO marvellous to see you here.'

Liah spun round at the familiar voice to see her old Cambridge University acquaintance, Clara Turnbull, approaching her through the throng of people gathered in the ornate rose garden of the Zokari embassy in London's Mayfair. The torchlight gleamed off the woman's elaborate blonde chignon.

Liah's heart sank and the nerves in her stomach twisted.

The daughter of a British investment banker, Clara had been one of Colin's friends, not hers, but it didn't surprise Liah in the slightest to see the woman at the exclusive gathering being given in Kamal's honour by the Zokari ambassador.

She forced herself to smile and accept the obligatory air kisses. 'Clara, why am I not surprised to see you here?' she managed, trying not to let the nerves that had besieged her for the last week show.

She was used to being at lavish diplomatic gatherings like this one, where champagne and diplomacy flowed freely and important relationships were forged between nations under the guise of small talk. After all, she'd been brought up in this rarefied world and she knew how it worked.

Unlike Kamal. She had been watching him all evening on the other side of the garden, looking tense and irritated in his formal suit, after he had been whisked away from her side as soon as their engagement had been lavishly toasted.

Her heart pulsed with sympathy for him.

One of the many things she had discovered about Kamal in the past week was that he hated small talk, almost as much as he hated wearing a suit, because he saw no need to fit in. And he didn't drink alcohol, so he couldn't even use its effects to relax as he was paraded round like a prize—something she also knew he hated.

She wondered if he had really factored in what his position would entail when he had worked so hard to achieve it. Because during the whirlwind activities of the past week—as they'd done a whistle-stop tour of the commerce capitals of Europe, attending a series of equally lavish events, then tearing each other's clothes off as soon as they were alone each evening—she had seen the toll it had taken on his patience and control.

She knew from the conversations they had late at night, after they'd made mad, frantic love—his ferocious need for her as intoxicating as listening to the plans for his country she had never expected him to share with her—that all he had ever really wanted was to see Zokar thrive. And to evolve the more tra-

ditional customs which he felt held the country back
from achieving its full potential.

Even though his was mostly a ceremonial position,
she knew he'd spent his own money, not just restoring
the prince's palace to its former glory but also invest-
ing in Zokar's ageing infrastructure, its education and
health system. He understood very well the importance
of attracting more investment to the region, but what he
didn't understand—and, she had discovered in the last
week, had no aptitude for whatsoever—was how to be
diplomatic. To pretend to be one of the ruling elite. The
fact Kamal did not consider himself one of *them*, and
had no desire to pretend otherwise, didn't help either.

'Darling, I heard you were going to be here with
your princely new desert hottie, and I could not resist angling for an invitation,' Clara supplied, sending
her an arch look which made Liah want to punch the
woman on the nose.

Desert hottie? What the actual...?

'Kamal's not a piece of meat, Clara, he's incredibly
intelligent and erudite.' Something else Liah had discovered more about in the past week. 'And he's also
the heir presumptive to a vast and extremely prosper-
ous desert kingdom. Not to mention a successful businessman.'

She felt the little trickle of shame which had assailed
her more than once over the past seven days. Hadn't
she herself objectified Kamal once, even considered
him unsophisticated? But her first impression had finally come crashing down all the way during their tour.
He was blunt, yes, and had no time for the insincere

niceties used in the name of diplomacy. But that was because he did not suffer fools and dealt with everyone with the same honesty and integrity—no matter their station in life.

She'd been there to smooth his path, and it had flattered her when he had seemed grateful for her presence. She'd loved the thought he needed her there, that he genuinely valued her input and expertise. Who knew she had more diplomatic skills than she'd ever realised?

They'd been feted in Italy, having toured a series of vineyards and olive farms, where the minerals which Kamal's company had discovered in the dry river beds of the Zokar foothills were proving so effective as a natural insecticide. They'd also received a lavish welcome in France, where they had toured a series of factories and wineries, and where a reception had been held in their honour amid the Baroque splendour of the Palace of Versailles.

Kamal had conversed in faltering but functional French with a host of dignitaries and businessmen about the investment potential for them in Zokar's vast mineral wealth. But he had been more than happy to let her handle the more detailed conversations because she was fluent in the language. Not to mention all the small talk necessary to finesse a commitment out of cagey investors and politicians.

They wanted what Kamal had to sell and he knew it, which was why he had no patience with attempts to finesse a better deal out of Zokar. But he had relied on her to soothe ruffled feathers. They actually made a good team, out of bed as well as in it.

'Don't be insulted, honey,' Clara said in a mocking tone that couldn't help but be insulting. 'I'm sure he's very smart but, more to the point, he's got a raw charisma which I bet makes the down time between diplomatic engagements very rewarding.'

Liah stiffened, not liking the woman's tone at all. As if Kamal really were a piece of meat.

'No wonder you dumped Colin—if you had this hunk waiting in the wings to propose,' Clara continued, apparently oblivious to Liah's rising indignation. 'Or was this an arranged marriage?' she continued. 'If so, you lucked out, being forced to marry *him*.' She finished, her openly lascivious gaze devouring Kamal as she made typically ill-informed assumptions about the culture and traditions of Liah's home region.

'I'm not being forced to marry anyone.' Liah glared, the fact she wasn't actually going to marry Kamal at all not stopping her from wanting to defend their union.

'Oh my, so it's a love match?'

Clara's mocking gaze shocked Liah for a moment. What was going on here? Did Clara have some kind of axe to grind?

'That was fast. I thought you only broke up with Colin a few months ago?'

'It was six months ago, actually, and Colin and I were never that serious.'

'Yes, I know,' Lara said, her tone becoming laser-sharp as her gaze raked over Liah. 'You do know he was sleeping with me at uni while waiting for the Crown Princess to finally get off her pedestal?'

'W-what?' The word came out on a shocked gasp.

She'd known Colin was a jerk and had got over his betrayal long ago. He'd used her, and she was pathetically grateful now she had never slept with him. But something about the fact she had been stupid enough to ever consider sleeping with him made her feel ashamed now. And like an idiot.

What a shallow fool she'd been, believing his lies and flattery. Thinking he cared for her when he never had. Had everyone known he was using her, except herself?

'He always insisted you were frigid, but I guess that was just his pride talking. From the way your new guy looks at you, it's pretty obvious you're keeping him well satisfied.' Clara's chuckle seemed bitter somehow, but behind it was a sadness that defused Liah's anger until all that was left was pity…and the humiliating pulse of heat at the thought of exactly how well-satisfied Kamal was keeping her.

Was she using him too? Because she was enjoying pretending to be his fiancée a bit too much. The engagement didn't feel like a lie any more—at least, not completely—ever since they had arrived in Europe and he had been happy to rely on her, to defer to her whenever his natural brusqueness created waves. And then there were the nights when he had come to her suite or dragged her into his and ravaged her with the same power and passion he had used ever since that first night. As if everything about her fascinated and excited him.

And her response to him was equally as ravenous.

How did he know just how to taste her, to touch her,

to caress and cajole her, to make her beg for more? Only last night he had thrust into her from behind as he'd caressed her in the shower, turning her body into a mass of molten sensations.

She had become obsessed with him, that much was obvious. Obsessed not just with what he could do to her body, but how he could make her feel. As if she was being worshipped on the one hand, but in charge of her own pleasure on the other. He challenged her, provoked her at every turn, demanding more than she had ever thought she would be willing or even capable of giving... But he also enjoyed it when she challenged and provoked him too. He wasn't afraid of her reckless- ness, wasn't scared of her demands, because he could be equally as ruthless and demanding.

They were equals in the best sense of the word.

'Colin was a jerk,' Liah said softly, knowing how true that was now. Colin hadn't been a man—he had been a spoilt, entitled boy. Kamal, on the other hand, had been a man from a very young age, too young an age in many ways. But he'd turned all his disadvan- tages into advantages, his powerlessness into strength, and he wielded it with a dignity and integrity that most people in his position could only dream of.

'We're both lucky to be rid of him,' she added. Al- though she could barely remember Colin any more. The heartache he'd once caused her felt little more than an irritating ripple now compared to everything she had begun to feel for Kamal.

Clara nodded, toasting her with her champagne glass. 'Ain't that the truth?' she said, then downed the contents in one go. 'I always wanted to hate you, you know,' she went on, surprising Liah with her candour. 'But, FYI, you didn't miss a thing with Colin. He was as selfish in bed as he was out of it.' So saying, she melted into the crowd just as a large hand landed on Liah's waist.

'Who is that woman? And what did she say to you?' Kamal stared down at her, his eyes flashing with barely concealed fury.

'It's nothing, Kamal, I'm fine,' she said, stupidly touched he seemed so angry on her behalf and also oddly exhilarated by the protective look in his eyes—and the fact he must have spotted her distress from the other side of the garden and come charging to her rescue. Why didn't that possessive tone bother her any more?

'Clara's someone I knew at Cambridge,' she added.

He lifted his hand to skim a callused thumb down her cheek. She shivered, as always far too aware of the slightest touch. His hand landed on her collarbone, both intimate and somehow protective, his gaze riveted to hers as that dangerous thumb continued to rub her pulse point. 'I do not like her. She has made you unhappy.'

'I'm fine,' she repeated, aware of the other guests staring.

A camera flashed nearby as the official photographer took their picture. The photos would be in all the papers tomorrow—because, much to her consternation, in the last week she and Kamal and their whirlwind romance had become a favourite subject of the celebrity media all over Europe. For once she didn't feel like a total fraud, though. 'Honestly, she just reminded me how glad I am I'm no longer at uni.'

He nodded. 'Who is Colin?' he asked, his tone lowering.

Uh-oh, so he'd heard some of their conversation. Liah stiffened, the probing look in his eyes making the shame and humiliation return.

'He's nobody,' she said truthfully. Because Colin meant nothing to her now, and he never really had. To think she had once tried to kid herself she could love a man like that, when what she felt for the man in front of her was so much more intense after only a couple of weeks in his company.

She was drawn to Kamal even though his arrogance was as infuriating as his dominant, taciturn nature. The sexual connection between them was so tangible, so fierce, she could feel herself getting moist—her body already preparing to accept his—while they were at an event crowded with people.

But the connection she and Kamal shared had become so much more than that. He respected her, even as he challenged her. He needed her, more than even her family. Why did that suddenly seem so much more seductive than his incendiary ability to make her climax on demand?

'Is he the fool who did not take your virginity when he had the chance?' he asked.

Oh, for the love of...

Fire leapt into her cheeks as her skin became hot. 'Kamal, how about we don't talk about this here?'

She'd never considered herself to be shy, but something about the way he was looking at her, with both rich appreciation and grim determination, made her feel brutally exposed.

He nodded. Then gripped her hand and proceeded to drag her through the crowd towards the gated entrance to the garden and the steps back into the embassy.

'Kamal, where are you going? We're the guests of honour tonight and the event's not finished.'

'It is for us.' He threw the words over his shoulder, the autocratic reply unbearably compelling. 'I wish to know why that woman upset you, and if we cannot talk here, we will do it in private.'

The last thing she wanted to do was talk about Clara and Colin. Short of creating a scene, though, she didn't have much of a choice. But as he marched through the crowd, ignoring anyone who tried to waylay them, she found her heart ricocheting into her throat. When had she begun to find his arrogance so compelling?

The Zokari ambassador approached them. Kamal ignored him too and ploughed on to the exit as Liah threw a few parting pleasantries over her shoulder... From the indulgent smiles and shocked expression on the faces of many of the guests, most of them probably assumed he was marching her off to seduce her.

Dignified, much?

Leaving the scent of roses, the chill of the evening air and the flicker of torchlight behind them, Kamal strode into the embassy and along the darkened corridors of the empty residence to lead her up the stairs to their adjoining suites.

'For goodness' sake, Kamal. Every single person there will think we've run off to have sex. And our sudden exit is bound to be reported in tomorrow's press,' she said breathlessly, trying desperately to sound reasonable. And to actually care what anyone else thought, while her insides were in turmoil and the pulse point in her sex was about to explode if he didn't touch her soon. *Very* soon.

Since when had she begun to find his ruthlessness, his dictatorial behaviour, so arousing? After taking the stairs two at a time, trying to keep up with his long strides—not easy in four-inch heels—she struggled to catch her breath, desperate to control the deep pulse of yearning which felt like so much more than desire.

Leading her into his room, Kamal slammed the door behind them and swung her round to face him. Her back in the plunging gown touched the cool wood of the door. But that wasn't the reason she shivered as he tucked a knuckle under her chin and tipped her face up to meet his gaze.

'This Colin, he is the man you *wished* to take your virginity?' he asked, his voice rough with something that sounded oddly like regret, his amber eyes dark and intense, but also full of an emotion which matched her own.

Why did she feel as if she were at the centre of a gathering storm? A storm she couldn't control but had no desire to escape.

'*What?* No!' she said, struggling to get a grip on the conversation when everything inside her was yearning for… It wasn't sex…or not *just* sex. When had she begun to want more? To need more? They'd only been together a couple of weeks. And yet the connection between them had begun to feel so strong, so important, ever since their night together in the encampment— maybe even before that. How could they have built something so vivid, so all-consuming, so quickly? How could this stark, stern, unknowable man feel like her soul mate?

'But he is the reason you will not marry me. Yes?' Kamal demanded, his gaze filled with the same yearning as her own.

'No, Kamal.' She touched his cheek, shocked to see the flash of intense longing in his gaze.

Was this more for him too? Why hadn't she seen it before now?

'Why, then, will you not make this engagement real?' he demanded, his voice raw with desperation. 'If it is not him, who is it?'

'It's too soon, Kamal,' she said weakly. 'We hardly know each other,' she murmured, trying to cling to practical considerations, but even those felt like lies now, pale, cowardly excuses.

'You know more of me, more of my past, than anyone alive,' he said, so simply her heart ached for him. He moved his head to bite into the swell of flesh under her thumb, the soft nip sending sensation shooting through her body. A sob of desire issued from her lips. He pressed a hand over hers, to kiss the tender flesh, then turned to her again, trapping her in that smouldering gaze.

'I know all the ways to make you ache, to make you

beg. We are a team, Liah. We could rule together, both Narabia and Zokar. With you by my side, I feel whole for the first time in my life.'

Her heart hammered her chest wall as his urgent words, the fierce yearning in his voice and the approval in his eyes struck down all the insecurities she had lived with for so long.

She had always been terrified of one day taking the Narabian throne, terrified of trying to live up to her father's and mother's legacy. But it suddenly occurred to her, they had not done it alone. What if Kamal was right? What if they could rule together too, bind their two countries?

But, as her heart thundered against her ribs and her pulse raced, she knew such practical considerations had nothing to do with the emotions battering her as she looked into those dark eyes and saw a man she wanted with every part of herself.

I don't just desire him. I don't just want to rule with him by my side... I love him. For who he is...who he has made himself...against all the odds. And because I know he could love me too. Not just the princess I am, the queen I will be one day, but who I am inside—the reckless, impulsive, insecure me, with all my imperfections. All my flaws.

Because Kamal had seen every one of those flaws in the short time they'd known each other and he still wanted to marry her.

He sank his face into her hair and kissed her neck, exploiting the spot where her pulse hammered—the place he knew would drive her wild.

He grasped her waist, tugging her against the immense ridge in his trousers—the evidence of how much he wanted her, how much he needed her—and turned the storm of emotion into a tsunami in her chest.

I love him. How can it be too soon?

Hadn't her own parents married each other after only a few weeks? she reasoned frantically, as she heard the zip of her gown releasing. He shoved the satin sheath down and unhooked her bra to free her breasts with ruthless efficiency.

She stood before him, naked now except for the thin swatch of lace covering her molten sex.

His tempestuous gaze roamed over her quivering flesh, then he moaned and bent to capture one turgid nipple in voracious lips. She shuddered, shocked by the sensation shimmering down as he tugged, nipped, suckled—first one swollen peak then the other. Her breath came out in ragged pants as she threaded her fingers into his silky hair, dragging him closer. She arched her back, forcing her breast into his mouth to ease the torment, desperate to satisfy the need.

He dragged himself back to throw off his jacket and rip off the shirt and tie. Buttons popped, the desire in his eyes flaring.

Then, to her astonishment, he sank to his knees, pressing his face to the apex of her thighs and drew in an unsteady breath.

'You smell so sweet to me, Kaliah…' He groaned as she clasped his head.

Then he lifted one of her legs over his shoulder, forcing her back against the door, exposing her molten sex completely. She shivered, vulnerable and yet so sure. Ripping aside the soaked gusset of her panties, he swept his tongue into the slick folds.

She cried out, her head bumping the door, her whole body on fire now as he licked at the stiff nub...too much and yet not enough.

She groaned, the sensations merging, the vice at her core cinching tight, and tighter still. 'Please, Kamal, please...'

He glanced up at her, ceasing the exquisite torture, leaving her wanting, waiting, desperate. His gaze locked on her face, dark with demand and desperation. 'Say you will marry me, Kaliah. Say you will become my queen?'

'Okay.' The word was released in a staggered rush, the emotion like a wave barrelling towards her. So right, so true. 'Yes, I'll marry you. I love you, Kamal.'

He went still. And for one bright, beautiful moment she thought he would say it too. Surely, he must feel it too? But, instead of saying the words, he nodded then lurched to his feet, dislodging her leg.

She stood, shuddering, naked, vulnerable, as she watched him release the huge erection from his trousers. Lifting her easily in his arms, he lowered her, impaling her on the thick girth.

She groaned, the stretched feeling one she recognised as she struggled to adjust to his size. But this time it felt so much more overwhelming.

He hadn't said it. But did that really matter? she thought vaguely, her mind dazed, her emotions so raw. He would say it soon, when he was ready.

The pleasure built again with startling speed as he began to move, massaging that tender spot inside her he had exploited so many times before. But this time the pleasure was harsher, swifter, more devastating. She could hold none of herself back from him and the brutal onslaught.

She clung to his heavily muscled shoulders as she tried to find purchase, to find her equilibrium again. But, as her fingers brushed over the tell-tale ridges he had let no one see but her, she found herself torn adrift, with only him to centre her.

Her sobs echoed off the lavish antique furniture, the bright lights of the city outside nothing more than a haze as her vision blurred. His harsh grunts matched the rhythmic thuds of her back hitting the door as she soared into another dimension. Not just her body, but her mind, her soul and every part of her heart.

The pleasure burst in fast, vicious waves, rolling through her, barrelling over her, shooting her into the abyss. She slumped against him, her face buried against his neck, her chest imploding, her heart shattering, as he shouted out his own release.

As the afterglow washed through her, she wrapped limp arms around his neck—his length still firm, still there inside her—and held him tight.

Even if he didn't love her yet, she loved him enough for both of them. And they would work this out together. Agreeing to marry Kamal for real was madness, on one level, but it felt so right, so perfect, on another as he carried her into his bed chamber, laid her on the king-sized bed then draped the covers over her.

She gathered the rest of her strength to lift up on her elbows as she watched him finish undressing in the moonlight then climb in beside her.

'Shouldn't I head back to my own room?' she asked. They never spent the whole night together in case their staff caught them in the morning.

But he simply grunted, yanking her into his embrace. 'No,' he said as she rested her head on his broad shoulder, loving the feel of his strong arms around her. 'You are mine now, always,' he said with typical possessiveness.

She smiled as she drifted into a deep sleep.

And you're mine, Kamal. Even if you don't know it yet.

'I love you, Kamal.'

The whispered words echoed in Kamal's head as he stared at the grandiose moulding on the ceiling of the London embassy's master bedroom, listened to the soft snores of the woman in his arms and tried to think past the raw emotion crushing his ribs like a boulder.

Kaliah's declaration was not something he wanted, not something he knew what to do with. Not something he even understood. But he couldn't seem to deny the deep feeling of satisfaction—even stronger than when she had agreed to marry him—when she had said those words to him.

The hope in her eyes, though, had stunned him more. How could she be so open, so trusting, so sure?

He frowned, his heartbeat accelerating to reverberate in the quiet room.

When she had first suggested this fake engagement to appease her father, he had been furious. He did not need a fake queen, damn it, he needed a real one. And he did not require her protection, nor did he require her pity. But he had been forced to resign himself to the subterfuge. Not least because he knew he was not ready, *yet*, to let her go. They still had unfinished business.

Plus, a part of him had marvelled at her intelligence and her bravery, not only in standing up to her father, but also standing up to him when Khan had arrived at the encampment.

That she had seen his scars and had not been repulsed had also had a profound effect on him—even if it was one he had refused to truly acknowledge up until now. But he admitted now, as his breathing finally evened out and his mind blurred, that enough of that brutalised boy remained to want to wallow in her approval.

The purpose of bringing her with him to Europe had been to finally put this need, this constant longing, to rest. But, each night he took her, the need only increased—her instant and enthusiastic response to him only fuelling the desire like dry grass in the path of a wildfire.

He wanted her, all the damned time. But worse was the discovery of how much easier it would be to negotiate this new world he had entered with her by his side. He had expected her to condescend to him, to perhaps even be disgusted at his lack of diplomacy, his intense dislike of the games politicians played. But instead she had encouraged and supported him. Not only did he not speak any of the western languages with any skill apart from English, but he was a man used to plain speaking, to giving orders and having them obeyed, which meant dealing with bureaucrats, politicians and diplomats was nothing short of excruciating.

But, every time he'd become frustrated or irritated, she had stepped in to help. Not only that, but she had listened with interest when he had spoken of his plans for Zokar.

Not just listened, but encouraged.

And slowly, as the need built each night, and having her by his side each day became more of a necessity, a thought had begun to form in his head...

He wanted Kaliah Khan to become his queen—for real. But even so he had hesitated. He'd had no desire to ask her for her hand and be rejected again... Because now it would have hurt so much more than just his pride.

And so he had side-lined the thought. Until he had seen her face fall while talking to that woman at the reception tonight, and as he'd got close enough to hear the mention of another man's name.

Anger had hit first. Who was this woman who had hurt her? But worse had been the spurt of jealousy and fear. As he had dragged her up to their suite, he hadn't been able to think past it.

She'd responded to him as she always did, with fierce desire, genuine hunger and complete honesty, and suddenly he had needed to make this commitment real. To ensure he didn't lose her.

When she had told him she loved him, he had been humbled and shocked.

But most of all he had been scared.

Because as he had claimed her, pouring his seed into the tight clasp of her body, wanting to imprint himself on every part of her, to brand her as his always, to seal the bargain they had made, he knew he would never be able to let her go…

CHAPTER TWELVE

'DAD? I'M SO glad you called. I take it you and Mum got the official invitation to our wedding this weekend?' Liah said down the phone, her heart galloping at the sound of her father's voice.

'Yes, we received it by special messenger this morning, Liah,' he said, his tone grave.

She clutched the handset. His voice sounded so familiar and yet somehow so far away, her heart hurt as she stared at the water trickling down from the fountain in the courtyard of the palace's bridal suite in Zokar.

'I know you've always been impulsive, sweetheart,' he added. 'But surely this is a little fast, even for you?'

I know, right?

She swallowed the reply and the lump of panic that had been there for two days.

She and Kamal had only arrived back from London forty-eight hours ago, and she'd been more than a little stunned to realise plans were already in place for their wedding in less than four days' time. She'd assumed she would have more time…a lot more time…to adjust to the reality of the situation. And the fact she'd hardly had a chance to see Kamal since they'd returned, let alone speak to him, hadn't exactly helped ease her anxiety about the speed of the wedding.

She'd missed him, not just at night, but during the day too. She understood tradition demanded they remain separate now until the ceremony was conducted before sharing a bed in the palace. But why did everything have to be so rushed?

Ultimately, though, she had forced herself not to panic. Surely, these were normal wedding jitters? She'd made a solid commitment to Kamal in London. And her feelings for him had only increased during the last of their official assignments and the journey home.

Kamal had been protective of her, and possessive. And she knew he hated this enforced separation as much as she did. He'd said as much when the plans for the whirlwind wedding had been revealed—and her short period of isolation had begun.

'There is nothing I want more than to make you my wife, Kaliah, as soon as possible. Is this not what you want too?'

The intense emotion in his voice had made her nod before he'd left her at the door to her new quarters two days ago. Yes, it was all a bit fast, even for her, but she had no qualms about her decision. Not only was she looking forward to being with Kamal, she was also excited about her future role as Queen of Zokar. She had been given full command of hiring her own staff—and defining her own duties—but, more than that, Kamal had informed her through his executive assistant that, once they were wed, he would relinquish any claim to the Narabian throne.

She didn't want to relay any of her concerns about the speed of the marriage to her father, though. Because it would feel like a betrayal of Kamal, and the new phase of her life they would embark on together when she became Queen of Zokar.

'Well, you know me, I never do anything by halves.' She let out a laugh, which only felt slightly forced. 'I hope you'll all be able to come to the ceremony. Raif and Kasia have already confirmed they can attend with their oldest four,' she said, the nerves knotting in her stomach. 'And we're hoping Karim and Orla will be able to make it too, as they're in Zafar at the moment instead of Kildare. Unfortunately, Dane said Jamilla can't come, as she has some big event in Manhattan she can't shift,' she added, mentioning Karim's half-brother, a nightclub entrepreneur, and his wife, who ran a charitable foundation in New York. 'But Dane's coming with their three-year-old twins. By the way, why are there so many sets of twins in our family?' she added, her laugh sounding manic now even to her own ears as her father remained suspiciously silent. 'Seriously, I should probably be concerned.'

'Take a breath, Liah,' her father said, his voice finally stopping the stream of inane information.

'You are coming, aren't you?' she managed, the desperation in her voice impossible to hide.

'Of course,' he said.

'Thank God!' she blurted out. 'And William and Kasim and Rohaan?' she added, suddenly knowing she needed her brothers there too, to ground her. Un-shed tears scraped at her throat. She missed them all so much.

'Yes, they'll be coming too.'

She blinked to hold back the traitorous emotion making her chest feel tight.

Why did she feel unsteady, so unsure? This was silly. She'd agreed to this marriage. She loved Kamal. But the thought of seeing her father, her mother and the whole of her family made it all seem more real and that much more overwhelming.

'You don't have to go through with this if you're not ready, Liah,' her father said gently.

The words didn't even register at first, but when they did the strange combination of uncertainty and anxiety pressing on her chest morphed into something even more disturbing—panic. 'But...but I am ready,' she said.

'Are you sure, honey?' he said again, sounding con-cerned.

And suddenly she was a little girl again, with his strong arms around her as he held her on the saddle of her first pony, and as he let go, telling her not to go too fast over the jumps. Of course, she had gone too fast, and she'd fallen and broken her arm in the process. He'd raced to her side, picked her up and cradled her on his lap until the palace medical team had arrived. But he'd never chastised her. And neither had her mother.

They'd always stood by her, even when she'd made stupid mistakes.

But this isn't a mistake. It can't be.

'I know he needs to get married before his corona-tion ceremony next week or he risks losing his throne,' her father added. 'But you shouldn't feel pressured into agreeing to this marriage if you're not one hundred percent sure.'

'Sorry, what?' she said, her voice a squeak of dis-tress.

Had she heard that correctly? Surely she couldn't have?

'You didn't know?' Her father swore, the ugly, angry word making nausea well in Liah's gut.

Had Kamal lied to her? Why hadn't he told her he needed a wife to secure his throne? Was that why he'd asked her to make this engagement real, why the wed-ding had been scheduled so quickly? Had he used her, the same way Colin had used her?

He never said he loved you. And now you know why.

The bleak thought had the nausea bubbling under her breastbone. The hollow weight in her stomach was worse, because it was a feeling she remembered when she'd overheard Colin's making fun of her to his friends. But this time the weight was so much heavier…

Because she'd never loved Colin. Had never felt for him even a tiny part of what she felt for Kamal.

'Liah, I'm coming to get you,' her father snapped, sounding furious, and more than a little irrational. But something about his anger, the fiery temper, helped to calm her own panic—a bit. 'No way in hell are you marrying a man who can't be honest with you about something so funda—'

'Dad, it's okay, I knew.' She forced out the lie, de-

'Kaliah, what is it?' he asked, concerned by the emotion in her eyes.

'Kamal, we need to talk.' Her gaze flashed to the elders behind him, who Kamal could already hear whispering about the break with tradition her appearance had caused. 'In private,' she added pointedly.

'Leave us.' He threw the command over his shoulder, unable to take his eyes off Kaliah—the strange expression in her eyes, wary but also full of hope, starting to concern him.

The majority of the elders filed out while continuing to whisper in hushed tones, except Uttram. 'Your Highness, it is not appropriate that you speak to—'

'Leave us!' he shouted, his patience with the man at an end. Bowing obsequiously, the man finally left them alone.

The silence was oppressive. He could hear her ragged breathing and the thunder of his own heartbeat as he dragged in a greedy lungful of her scent. Desire pooled in his groin. But worse was the desperation, the yearning, which he had spent the last forty-eight hours trying to deny.

Why could he not control his need for this woman, not just in bed, but out of it too? The sight of her excited him in so many ways—but not all of them were sexual.

She tugged her arms free of his grip and stepped back. He plunged his empty hands into his pockets.

Folding her arms over her waist, her gaze sharpened.

'Why didn't you tell me you needed this marriage to happen now to secure your throne?'

He stiffened. He could hear only confusion in her

tone, not accusation or distress, but even so the guilt lodged in his chest.

'Because it was not relevant,' he said.

Her brow furrowed. 'That's nonsense, Kamal. Of course it's relevant, that's why the ceremony is happening this weekend and not six months from now, isn't it? Admit it.'

Of course, she was right about that, but admitting as much seemed pointless, and fraught with complications, so he changed tack. 'It is not relevant, because I would have wished for this marriage anyway,' he said, knowing it was the truth. 'You are everything I want and need as my queen.'

Instead of placating her, though, his declaration only seemed to disturb her, the expression on her face turning from confusion to consternation.

'As your queen?' she queried, searching his face, as if looking for something. 'What about as a woman?'

The hammer thuds of his heart dimmed a little. This question at least was very simple to answer. A slow smile spread as his gaze dipped to take in her high breasts and the flutter of her pulse in her collarbone. His mouth watered at the thought of kissing her there.

'As a woman, I want you very much,' he said. He lifted his hand from his pocket to wrap it around her arm and tug her against him, making her aware of the burgeoning erection. 'Do you wish me to prove it to you?'

Her breath released in a rush, her eyes darkening. He could scent her arousal, and the powerful desire surged.

She was his, she would always be his. Their chemistry was so strong, neither one of them could deny it.

But as he bent his head, intending to suckle the place on her neck he knew would make her melt, she braced her palms against his chest.

'Stop it, Kamal. I'm not talking about sex. I'm talking about love.'

'What?' he murmured, shocked by the deep yearning in her eyes, and the shimmer of hope.

He had seen it once before, when she had told him she loved him two days ago and had waited for his reply. Just as then, it struck fear into his heart.

He released her abruptly.

He couldn't have this conversation—not now, not yet—because he had no answer that would satisfy her. But nor did he wish to lie or make her promises he could not fulfil.

'I want to know, what do you really feel for me?' She said the words carefully, gently, without an ounce of entitlement but with a grim determination that told him there would be no ducking the truth a second time. 'Not as a queen, or as a...' the flush spread across her collarbone '...a—a sexual partner. I want to know if you love me, even a little bit. The way I love you.'

He stepped back to lean against his desk, studying her as he thrust his hands back into his pockets, contemplating what the hell to say. Her beautiful face was so expressive, so open, so transparent. It was one of the things he adored about her. But right now that devastating combination of hope and fear was crucifying him.

'It's not a difficult question, Kamal,' she said, her

gaze so intense now—looking for something he knew he could not give her—that the fear returned. 'Why is it so hard for you to answer it?'

Lie. Tell her what she wants to hear. Your throne depends on it.

The voice in his head demanded what he should say. The voice he had relied on as a boy to survive. The voice which had pushed him for so long to do and say whatever it took to get what he wanted, what he needed, to prosper and achieve his goals... But he could not get the necessary words out past the boulder of guilt and remorse growing in his throat.

He had lied before when he'd needed to... But he could not lie to her any more than he could fight off the pain in his chest at the sight of her distress.

Tugging his hand from his pocket, he brushed a thumb down the side of her face, needing to touch her, to feel that connection he could not put into words as he told her the truth.

'You are a romantic, Kaliah,' he said softly. *Because you can afford to be*, he thought silently. 'But love is simply a word,' he added. 'It means nothing tangible, nor is it something I require. Commitment is all that matters. Commitment and honesty.' He rested his hand on her shoulder, rubbing his thumb across the frantic pulse, willing her to understand, the pain in his chest increasing at the despair in her eyes. 'I wish you to be my wife, my queen. I wish you to have my children. To rule by my side. Is that not enough?'

'I see,' she whispered, her voice calm, but the expression in her eyes somehow broken. 'Thank you for being honest with me.'

He nodded. But, instead of feeling satisfaction at her measured response, his pulse continued to rage, the pain refusing to ease.

She blinked as a single tear spilled over her lid. The pain gathered, becoming all but unbearable. But he braced against it and the sudden urge to drag her into his arms, to make love to her and tell her anything and everything she wanted to hear to make her love him still.

It was better that she knew the truth about what he was capable of—and what he was not. Better that she accepted it.

Even so, as she swiped the drop away with a shaky fist and walked away from him, he could not shake the devastating feeling that enveloped him... Or the suspicion he might just have lost something more precious than the Zokari throne, and infinitely more rare than the perfect queen.

He forced himself not to dwell on it, not to allow foolish sensibilities to derail him during the sleepless night that followed, as the picture of her devastated expression, the depth of feeling in her eyes, woke him from nightmares.

But the whole fragile house of cards came crashing down the next morning when one of his advisers dashed into his bed chamber to deliver the news that the Crown Princess had left Zokar under cover of darkness with the assistance of one of her staff. And handed him a note.

> *I'm so sorry, Kamal. I can't marry you knowing there is no prospect you will ever love me. Love isn't just a word. Not to me. It's everything.*
> *I hope you don't lose your throne because of this, when I know what a good king you will be.*
> *Kaliah xx*

Agony broke open in his chest, but right beneath it was rage. She had dared to leave him. How could she have loved him and then left him to forfeit his throne? Scrunching up the note, he threw it across the room.

But the vicious anger drained away almost as quickly as it had come and the tearing agony remained, leaving him raw, shaky and…for the first time in his life…defeated.

He had lost everything…and he had no idea how to get it back.

CHAPTER THIRTEEN

'I LOVE HIM, but he doesn't love me. He doesn't even *want* to love me…' Liah scrubbed the tears off her cheeks, the skin smarting after all the tears she had already shed as soon as she'd arrived home—and her mother had wrapped her arms around her.

It had been a long, arduous journey overnight through the desert in the SUV she'd managed to liberate from the palace with help from her lady's maid, Maya. She was utterly exhausted now, not just from the physical toll of the eight-hour drive over the rough unforgiving terrain, but also from the emotional devastation Kamal had caused when she had confronted him about his motives…and he'd given her nothing.

She'd been such a fool to think he loved her. That he wanted her for herself, and not simply to keep his throne. What hurt more, though, was the thought that even up to the moment when he'd gone utterly still… staring at her after her question about his feelings had dropped into that awful, heavy silence and he'd said nothing for the longest time…she'd had so much hope. Hope that she'd misread the situation. That it had simply been a mistake. That she'd judged him too quickly. That he'd chosen her because he believed in her, because he believed in *them*. Not because he simply needed a convenient bride.

But then it had all come crashing down.

'You're a romantic, Kaliah.'

The derogatory note in his voice had hurt immeasurably. Because in it she'd heard that cruel judgement she remembered from the day he'd plucked her off her horse at the Race of Kings. And she had finally realised that, despite everything they had done together, everything they had shared, he still viewed her on some level as a privileged brat.

She'd had parents who loved her, who supported her, who cared what she did and who respected her judgement—who hadn't abandoned her and forced her to do everything alone. But was she supposed to prove her worth because she hadn't suffered as he had, hadn't had to overcome anything like the same obstacles, for the rest of her life?

Far worse than his judgement about her strength of character—which he had clearly decided would never be as strong as his—had been the shuttered look in his eyes when he'd told her all he wanted was a wife, a queen. Not a soul mate, not a kindred spirit, not someone to share his heart with—only his throne. And then she'd understood he would always hold a part of himself back…

She gulped in a breath, the wrenching sobs making her chest hurt as her mother held her tight and consoled her.

'Shh, Liah, you need to breathe,' her mother murmured against her hair, her calming scent so familiar.

Liah sucked in a breath past the constriction in her throat, gulped in air and tried to even her breathing. At last, the storm began to pass. Until the wrenching sobs turned to hiccups.

'You need to tell me exactly what he said, sweetheart,' her mother said, her warm caramel-coloured eyes so full of compassion and understanding, Liah struggled to hold down another round of sobs.

'H-he… H-he said love was just a word. Th-that it didn't *mean* anything.' Even now, sixteen hours later, the ignorance of such a statement made her chest hurt. 'Th-that he just wanted a wife and a queen and a mother to his children.'

The surge of indignation fortified her a little— enough to finally pull herself out of her mother's arms and sit up on the couch in the Queen's study. 'Can you believe it?' she added. 'L-like I'm some sort of royal brood mare. Seriously, Mum, can you imagine if Daddy had ever said something like that to you? It's so cruel and so chauvinist.'

Her mother sent her an easy smile Liah didn't understand. How exactly was her having her heart ground to dust even remotely amusing?

'Actually, Liah,' her mother said, her voice gentle, but that enigmatic smile still in place, 'It sounds very much like what your father *did* say to me when he first demanded I marry him.'

Liah blinked, astonished by her mother's confession. 'He *demanded* you marry him?' *What the heck?* 'You're not serious?'

Surely her mother had to be exaggerating, or joking? Or simply trying to make her feel better about Kamal's cruelty?

Her parents were a great love match, a wonderful partnership. Everyone said so. And she'd seen how good they were together every day of her life. Of course, they had the occasional argument, some of which got pretty heated, because they were both strong-willed people in their own way, but they would never deliberately hurt each other—the way Kamal had so callously hurt her.

But her mother didn't look as if she was joking. In fact, that annoying smile broadened as she cupped Liah's cheek and pushed the wet strands of her hair back from her face. 'I should probably come clean at this point and admit we only got married originally because I was pregnant with you.'

'W-what?' Liah's strangled reply bounced off the walls of the quiet office. 'But…that… That can't be true. You both adore each other.'

'We didn't always adore each other, Kaliah. Nor did we understand each other,' her mother said softly as Liah's stunned shock turned to incomprehension. 'The truth is, there were a lot of ups and downs in the early years,' her mother added, her tone warm with reminiscence, as if she were reciting a funny anecdote—instead of rewriting the whole history of Liah's childhood.

'In fact, I ran away from him too because I was so upset with him. But one thing I always knew was that he was a good man… A pushy, overbearing, dictatorial and arrogant one at times, but still a good man.'

'But…how did you get past a forced marriage?' Liah said, still so shocked she could hardly talk.

'Oh, it wasn't forced, more expedient,' her mother said, touching Liah's arm gently before the smile turned a bit wicked. 'And your father has always been super-hot, so he was very persuasive.'

'*Eww*, Mum, stop! I do not need that picture in my head,' Liah muttered, feeling like a teenager again, catching her parents necking enthusiastically when they were supposed to be totally asexual.

But something about the whole conversation had started to ease the fierce, stabbing pain under her breastbone that had been there ever since her showdown with Kamal.

'I still don't understand how you got past *having* to get married because of me,' she said, her curiosity getting the better of her.

'Well,' her mother replied, considering. 'Firstly, we discovered a lot of things about each other. For example, I discovered the extent of the abuse he had suffered,' her mother added, her expression sobering.

Liah knew her grandfather, the previous Sheikh of Narabia, had been a cruel ruler and a worse father— she knew he had kidnapped her father as a teenager from his mother in LA and had also disowned her uncle Raif when his mother had died in childbirth. But, because Sheikh Abdullah had died before Liah had been born, and her father had never spoken of him, she'd never really considered what that had all really meant.

Her mother continued. 'I discovered, because of his father's abuse and his mother's neglect, Zane had been forced to protect his feelings at all costs. Letting me in was incredibly painful for him, something it took me a while to appreciate.'

'That's so sad,' Liah murmured, her heart breaking for both of them.

'Yes, but the point is we figured it out. Eventually.' Her mother laughed, the soft, musical sound making Liah's sore heart pound. Her mother gripped Liah's hands and rubbed her thumbs across the skin. 'People can heal, Liah, but only if they want to enough, and if they are given the tools and space to do so.'

Liah met her mother's gaze, feeling oddly ashamed. Had she simplified and romanticised everything? Made too many demands on Kamal? She'd run away from him and as a result he might lose his throne. She'd thought he was judging her, but had she given enough consideration to what he had been through in his life before he had ever met her?

'From everything you've told me about Kamal, and the things he said to you, he sounds quite similar to your father in those early days,' her mother said softly. 'I'm not saying you should marry him, not even to help him keep his throne—that's not a reason to marry anyone. And your father is absolutely right, he should have told you the situation from the outset. But maybe you shouldn't write him off completely. It's obvious that, despite everything Kamal's said and done and the things he hasn't done or said, you still love him… What you have to ask yourself now is, do you want to throw those feelings away, or is it worth working on them with him? Because, make no mistake, marriage and relationships are hard work, especially the ones that last.'

She sighed. 'Love really is just a word, you know, he's right about that. It's what's behind it that matters. I can't tell you the number of times I've wanted to strangle your father because he was obtuse, or hot-headed or uncommunicative... But I never stopped wanting to do the work. And neither did he.'

Liah felt hope bubble in her chest again. But this time it felt so much more painful.

'But I'm not sure Kamal does want to do the work,' she said, still desperately unsure. Maybe she had been naïve, maybe she had over-simplified things, but how much evidence did she really have that Kamal saw her as more than a means to an end? 'He told me he didn't require love.'

Catherine nodded. 'It sounds to me like he's terrified.'

'Kamal? Are you joking?' Liah spluttered. 'He's even more overbearing and intimidating than Dad. I don't think he's ever been scared of anything in his life.'

'Are you certain of that?' her mother said, her gaze probing.

And suddenly Liah recalled the flicker of shame in his eyes when she had mentioned his scars. Was there still some of that boy inside him, who had been taught from such an early age he would always be alone, that he wasn't worthy of love, that he would never be cherished?

What if her mother was right and it wasn't that he couldn't love her…it was that he was terrified of loving anyone? Of trusting anyone to love him?

'Oh, no, I may have made a terrible mistake,' she murmured, the bubble of hope becoming a balloon.

Just as a confident smile tilted her mother's lips, Kaliah's aunt Kasia—the Princess of the Kholadi tribe—burst into the chamber, holding the hands of her two-year-old twins, Khalid and Sami. 'Liah, you need to come to Zane's study. Someone just arrived by helicopter and Zane's having a tough time preventing him from charging through the palace in search of you.'

'Kamal?' Liah murmured, that bubble of hope pressing against her larynx.

'If he's six and a half foot, and even more scarily intense than my husband when he's freaking out about me getting pregnant again, then that would be the guy,' Kasia replied with an easy smile. It was a running joke in the family—given Kasia and Raif had had three sets of twin births—that Raif was not in a good place whenever his petite wife became pregnant.

Liah rushed past her aunt and her cousins, unable to think about anything but the painful pressure in her chest. It didn't take her long to catch the sound of her father and her fiancé shouting at each other. She followed the commotion, pushing her way through the palace staff who had amassed by the door to the study, clearly eavesdropping. She burst into her father's study to see Kamal and her father going head to head.

She'd thought she would never see him again. Why had it not occurred to her until this moment, as he stood glaring at her father, his robes swirling around his long legs, his stance rigid, that it was the thought of *never* seeing him again which had hurt most of all?

'Kamal?' she gasped, breathless and stupidly euphoric.

He swung round, his gaze bright but also awash with pain. 'Kaliah, you must come back to me,' he rasped. He looked distraught, she realised, as she crossed the room towards him. His stance was so rigid, his eyes shadowed and so intense. This wasn't arrogance, this was fear. Just as her mother had said.

'You'll do no such damn thing, Liah,' her father interceded. 'This bastard has no right to—'

'Dad, stop talking!' She cut off her father's tirade, unable to detach her gaze from the man in front of her, the man she loved.

'What the...?' her father began.

'Dad, please, this isn't your business,' she said, finally managing to stop staring at the man who had come to mean so much to her in such a short space of time. 'Kamal and I need to talk in private.'

'How can it not be my business?' her dad demanded, temper replaced with confusion. 'He made you cry.'

Her heart swelled at the distress in her father's tone, symbolic of the unconditional love she had taken for granted her whole life.

Kamal has never had that kind of support. Don't underestimate how tough it is for him to let his guard down. To trust his feelings, as well as yours.

She nodded at her father. 'I know, but I can handle this now.'

Her father's gaze flicked from Kamal to her, and she could see he didn't want to leave her alone. But then her mother approached and took his arm.

'Give it up, Zane,' her mum said, placing a tender kiss on his jaw as she tugged him out of the room. 'She's not our little girl any more. She's her own woman. And she's got this.'

As the door closed behind her parents, Liah felt the balloon in her chest swell to impossible proportions. But she made herself swallow it down.

She could see the emotion on his face, knew that much more was going on than she had assumed. But one thing still held true—she had to stand her ground now, more than ever, for them both.

He stepped towards her and lifted his thumb, brushing it down the sore skin on her cheek, irritated by too many tears, tears he had caused.

'I am sorry, Kaliah. I did not mean to make you cry.'

She blinked, touched by the simplicity of the statement and the abject misery in his face. 'I know.'

'Why then did you run from me?' he asked, as if he really didn't know.

But she could see in his eyes, he did know. So she chose not to answer that question.

'I can't come back to you, Kamal. I won't. Not until you give me a good enough reason.'

He swore softly and stepped away, thrusting impatient fingers through his hair. She could see the flash of frustration, of temper even, but beneath it was the fear.

It was so clear and vivid to her now, she was amazed she hadn't seen it before.

Or perhaps he had always just been really good at hiding it from her—from everyone.

Her heart lifted a little more, the hope expanding again. That he couldn't hide it from her any more was definitely progress, of a sort.

He marched across the room and clasped his hands behind his back, staring out of the domed window at the Golden Palace's gardens and the high walls bathed in sunshine.

But something about that rigid stance—the tremor in his legs, the bunched muscles in his shoulders—made her see the darkness within. A darkness from which she could feel him struggling to break free. When he finally spoke, his voice a strained monotone, she sensed the battle he waged, even as she willed him to win.

'You asked me to love you,' Kamal said, feeling so broken inside, so needy, he was surprised his guts hadn't spilled out onto the priceless Afghan carpet on Zane Khan's study floor.

If he hadn't been so terrified, he would have been humiliated beyond bearing. But grovelling—even exposing all these horrifying new emotions—didn't seem so insurmountable any more if it would bring her back to him.

'But I don't even understand what that means,' he whispered, mortified by the rawness in his throat, the soreness behind his eyes. 'My earliest memory…before Hamid, before the orphanage…' he gulped, the memory still so painful '…is of the man who left me there. I think he must have been my father. But he did not love me. He cannot have done or he would not have left me. And if he could not…how can anyone?'

His father had left him. And he hadn't come back. He could have been a good boy, a better boy, but his father had never given him the chance to make amends for whatever he had done.

He had never cried, not since he'd been a little boy and he had begged for his father to return. Only to find all the tears in the world would not change what was.

But he had to strain every sinew now not to release the futile tears again as he waited for Kaliah's response to his confession.

He heard her footsteps, and braced himself for the pain of her leaving him again, but then her arms wrapped around his waist from behind and she pressed her face into his spine.

He slumped, the relief coursing through his body so immense, he was surprised he could still remain upright.

'It's okay, Kamal,' she said softly, her voice like a balm to that little boy, as well as the man he had become. 'You don't have to understand love—you don't even have to say you love me yet. All you have to do is let me know you need me. We can work everything else out as we go.'

He turned, clasped her shoulders and dug his fingers into her upper arms to lift her face to his. The tears glinting in her eyes crucified him, even as the tears he could not shed tore at his own heart. 'Really? This is all you require? How can it be enough?'

He wanted to believe her, wanted more than anything to pick her up and carry her to the nearest bed chamber so he could claim her, brand her as his for all eternity. But how could what he had given ever really be enough when she had given so much more?

A small smile creased her lips as she placed a trembling palm against his cheek. 'Because I love you, Kamal,' she said so simply, he felt his heart break open inside his chest and all the fear and confusion bleed out. 'I love your strength and your arrogance and your determination to protect me, and your desperate need never to show a weakness except to me.'

He covered her palm, absorbing the certainty in her words. She meant it. He could see that now with every fibre of his being.

He had no idea what he had done to deserve this, to deserve her, but he would not question it again—ever.

'And I think you love me too,' she added with a confidence, an arrogance, he had always adored, perhaps because it was more than a match for his own. 'You just don't know it yet. That's all.'

His heart exploded with joy as he lifted her off her feet then captured her mouth with his. The kiss was fierce, furious, but also tender.

A long time later, when they were finally forced to come up for air, she wiggled out of his arms and grasped his hand.

'Come on—we probably need to get back to Zokar

ASAP,' she said, attempting to tug him towards the door. 'We've got a wedding to plan and time is running out.'

He smiled as he resisted, charmed by her urgency. 'There is no need,' he said simply. 'The wedding is cancelled.'

'What?' Her eyebrows launched up her forehead, charming him even more. 'But what about your throne? Oh, my God…' She began to tug on his hand even harder. He remained firm. 'Kamal, stop messing about. For goodness' sake, we have to un-cancel the wedding. Pronto.'

'Shh, Kaliah.' He actually laughed, her frantic expression only making him adore her more. She would always have his back. Why had he not realised how much he needed that support from her until now? 'It's okay. We are not un-cancelling anything.'

'But the elders? The law? You have to be married to…'

'No, I do not,' he said, cradling her cheeks, loving the feel of her soft skin, the intoxicating scent of her. A scent he had become addicted to the first time he had inhaled it. 'If the elders choose another man to rule Zokar on this foolish technicality, that is on them.'

'You can't mean that!' she said, still sounding frantic.

'I do mean it,' he assured her, knowing he spoke the absolute truth. 'I will not jump through hoops for their benefit. You are too important to me. Our marriage is too important to me to rush into it before you are ready.'

'But I am ready now—totally. What difference does

a few extra days or weeks make if it means you can keep…?'

He pressed his finger to her lips to silence her panic. 'Do you not understand, Kaliah? It was never about that.' He sighed, the relief that he was finally able to be honest with himself, as well as her, almost palpable. 'I wished to rush you into marriage because I was scared of losing you. I see that now. The marriage ultimatum, the throne, was just a convenient excuse.' He shrugged. 'If they are foolish enough to discard me because of their asinine demands, then they are the idiots. Because I am by far the best man to be their king.'

'True.' Her lips quirked as the panic finally died, to be replaced by amusement and the same joy exploding in his heart. 'And you've also found the best woman to be their queen.'

'Also true.' He grinned, boosting her into his arms so he could take his own sweet time ravaging her lips.

Maybe the elders—especially Uttram and his followers—would see how good Kaliah and him would be as Zokar's rulers, maybe they would not. But, as she gripped his scalp and sunk into the kiss, the joy streaking through his body became turbo-charged.

Because the only kingdom he really *had* to rule now—and always—was the kingdom of Kaliah Khan's heart.

EPILOGUE

'YOU WERE SPECTACULAR TODAY, Kaliah. I am so proud to have you as my wife, my partner, my queen.'

Liah sighed as Kamal's lips brushed her nape. She covered the hands he pressed into her stomach with her own. Her heart beat a giddy tattoo in her chest, as it had been doing all day—ever since she had stood before a crowd of people she loved and respected and had declared her loyalty to this strong, commanding man and his kingdom, while he'd declared his loyalty to hers.

She blinked furiously as he kissed the pulse point in her neck, which always made her ache, and stared down at the enchanted garden in the Golden Palace's courtyard where she had once dreamed of finding a prince to love.

A watery smile lifted her lips. Today's ceremony had been part of the week-long wedding celebrations that had started five days ago in Zokar, not just to make their marriage official but also to link their two kingdoms, as Kaliah had taken her place beside Kamal on his country's throne and they'd been declared joint heirs to her parents' throne in Narabia.

The ceremony had been over six months in the making, with Kamal—intractable man that he was—insisting he did not want to stake a claim to her father's throne. In the end, she'd had to make him see that she had no desire to lead Narabia without him when the time came. But the good news was, her father and mother didn't look as if they were about to relinquish the throne any time soon, the recollection of their proud, happy smiles this afternoon making the emotion swell in her throat.

'What are you thinking?' Kamal murmured as he turned her in his arms.

She smiled, reaching up to place her palms on the rough stubble that had grown on his cheeks during the long day of official engagements. 'That I'm ridiculously proud to finally have you as my husband,' she said, lifting up on tiptoes to press her lips to his.

His hands grasped her waist in her beaded gown as he bent to take her mouth in a firm, possessive kiss. Need sparked and throbbed in her belly, right beside the flicker of excitement and anticipation at the news she had waited five interminable days to give him.

They'd been too tired and busy for her to find the right time ever since she had taken the test—the schedule of engagements and ceremonies to celebrate their union in both kingdoms nothing short of punishing. And, anyway, she'd wanted to wait until she was at the Golden Palace, in her childhood home—where all her dreams of love and romance had begun.

Kamal was nothing like the man she'd envisioned falling in love with one day. He was far too forthright and demanding, far too intense and masculine, far too vivid and vibrant… He made the Prince Charming of her daydreams seem pale, insubstantial and, frankly, exceedingly dull in comparison.

'Good,' he announced with a possessive huff, before scooping her into his arms. 'Because now I intend to get you out of that dress which has been driving me wild all evening and make you my queen in the only way that counts.'

She laughed as he marched into their bed chamber but, as he placed her beside the bed and set about divesting her of said gown, she clasped his hands. 'Wait, Kamal.'

'What? Why?' he asked, his impatient frown only making her love him more. She hoped that fierce need would never dim…

'I have something to tell you…' She hesitated as her heart throbbed into her throat.

He cradled her face in one callused palm, his thumb brushing away the tear that slipped down her cheek.

'What is it, Kaliah?' he asked, that flash of fear something she hoped to erase completely one day.

She swallowed, the emotion all but choking her.

She'd planned this moment so carefully over the last five days—exactly what she would say and how she would say it—but it all suddenly seemed like too much. They were entering another brand-new phase of their lives together, after only having just embarked on the last one and, as much as she knew Kamal wanted this, she wasn't sure if he wanted it right now.

'Whatever it is, we will fix it together,' he said, still

stroking her cheek, his face a mask of confusion now, and determination…and love.

Oh, for goodness' sake, Liah, just say it. You're scaring him.

'I'm pregnant!' she blurted out with a great deal less finesse than she had planned.

His eyes widened with shock, and then his gaze darted down to her stomach.

'You…? Y-you are having our child?' His expression was filled with awe as his gaze met hers.

She nodded, her stomach bouncing as he pressed a hand to where their baby grew.

'I found out on Monday. I guess my contraception must have failed when I had that bout of food poisoning last month…' She began to babble. 'I know we didn't plan it just yet, and it's going to be a lot to take on with all our new responsibilities, and the US trade tour next…'

'Shh…' he said then, to her astonishment, he sunk to his knees and pressed his cheek to her belly as his arms wrapped around her hips.

She stroked his silky hair, feeling the tremble of fierce emotion.

'Kamal, is everything okay?' she asked, her voice thick with tears now.

He looked up at her at last, his gaze dark and intense—and so full of joy, she had to wipe away the tears now streaming down her cheeks.

'Yes, everything is much, much better than okay,' he said.

Then he surged to his feet, lifted her into his arms and swung her around with a whoop of triumph.

Her laughter joined his deep chuckles as he set her back on her feet at last…and the fierce joy spread like wildfire in her heart.

* * * * *

*If you enjoyed Kamal and Kaliah's story
you might like to read Heidi Rice's other titles
that are linked by the Khan family:*

Zane and Catherine in
Carrying the Sheikh's Baby

Raif and Kasia in
Claimed for the Desert Prince's Heir

Karim and Orla in
Innocent's Desert Wedding Contract

Dane and Jamilla in
Banished Prince to Desert Boss

#4105 THE BABY BEHIND THEIR MARRIAGE MERGER
Cape Town Tycoons
by Joss Wood

After one wild weekend with tycoon Jude, VP Addison must confess a most unprofessional secret...she's pregnant! But Jude has a shocking confession of his own: to inherit his business, he *must* legitimize his heir—by making Addi his bride!

#4106 KIDNAPPED FOR THE ACOSTA HEIR
The Acostas!
by Susan Stephens

One unforgettable night with Alejandro leaves Sienna carrying a nine-month secret! But before she has the chance to confess, he discovers the truth and steals her away on his superyacht. Now, Sienna is about to realize how intent Alejandro is on claiming his child...

#4107 ITALIAN NIGHTS TO CLAIM THE VIRGIN
by Sharon Kendrick

Billionaire Alessio can think of nothing worse than attending another fraught family event alone. So, upon finding Nicola moonlighting as a waitress to make ends meet, they strike a bargain. He'll pay the innocent to accompany him to Italy...as his girlfriend!

#4108 WHAT HER SICILIAN HUSBAND DESIRES
by Caitlin Crews

Innocent Chloe married magnate Lao for protection after her father's death. They've lived separate lives since. So, when she's summoned to his breathtaking Sicilian castello, she expects him to demand a divorce. But her husband demands the opposite—an heir!

HPCNMRA0423

#4109 AWAKENED BY HER ULTRA-RICH ENEMY
by Marcella Bell

Convinced that Bjorn, like all wealthy men, is up to no good, photojournalist Lyla sets out to prove it. But when her investigation leads to an accidental injury, she's stranded under her enemy's exhilarating gaze...

#4110 DESERT KING'S FORBIDDEN TEMPTATION
The Long-Lost Cortéz Brothers
by Clare Connelly

To secure his throne, Sheikh Tariq is marrying a princess. It's all very simple until his intended bride's friend and advisor, Eloise, is sent to negotiate the union. And Tariq suddenly finds his unwavering devotion to duty tested...

#4111 CINDERELLA AND THE OUTBACK BILLIONAIRE
Billionaires of the Outback
by Kelly Hunter

When his helicopter crashes, a captivating stranger keeps Reid alive. Under the cover of darkness, a desperate intimacy is kindled. So, when Reid is rescued and his Cinderella savior disappears, he won't rest until he finds her!

#4112 RIVALS AT THE ROYAL ALTAR
by Julieanne Howells

When the off-limits chemistry that Prince Sebastien and Queen Agnesse have long ignored explodes...the consequences are legally binding! They have faced heartbreak apart. But if they can finally believe that love exists...it could help them face their biggest trial *together*.

Get 4 FREE REWARDS!

We'll send you 2 FREE Books plus 2 FREE Mystery Gifts.

FREE
Value Over
$20

Both the **Harlequin® Desire** and **Harlequin Presents®** series feature compelling novels filled with passion, sensuality and intriguing scandals.

YES! Please send me 2 FREE novels from the Harlequin Desire or Harlequin Presents series and my 2 FREE gifts (gifts are worth about $10 retail). After receiving them, if I don't wish to receive any more books, I can return the shipping statement marked "cancel." If I don't cancel, I will receive 6 brand-new Harlequin Presents Larger-Print books every month and be billed just $6.30 each in the U.S. or $6.49 each in Canada, a savings of at least 10% off the cover price, or 6 Harlequin Desire books every month and be billed just $5.05 each in the U.S. or $5.74 each in Canada, a savings of at least 12% off the cover price. It's quite a bargain! Shipping and handling is just 50¢ per book in the U.S. and $1.25 per book in Canada.* I understand that accepting the 2 free books and gifts places me under no obligation to buy anything. I can always return a shipment and cancel at any time by calling the number below. The free books and gifts are mine to keep no matter what I decide.

Choose one: ☐ **Harlequin Desire**
(225/326 HDN GRJ7)

☐ **Harlequin Presents Larger-Print**
(176/376 HDN GRJ7)

Name (please print)

Address   Apt. #

City   State/Province   Zip/Postal Code

Email: Please check this box ☐ if you would like to receive newsletters and promotional emails from Harlequin Enterprises ULC and its affiliates. You can unsubscribe anytime.

Mail to the Harlequin Reader Service:
IN U.S.A.: P.O. Box 1341, Buffalo, NY 14240-8531
IN CANADA: P.O. Box 603, Fort Erie, Ontario L2A 5X3

Want to try 2 free books from another series? Call 1-800-873-8635 or visit www.ReaderService.com.

HDHP22R3

HARLEQUIN
PLUS

Try the best multimedia subscription service for romance readers like you!

Read, Watch and Play.

Experience the easiest way to get the romance content you crave.

Start your **FREE TRIAL** at
www.harlequinplus.com/freetrial.